PRAISE FOR
THE PARKER NOVELS

"The master thief is back in the game . . . . Parker has not lost his touch—or his nerve . . . . In a world of warped values, an honest crook like Parker is a true treasure."
—Marilyn Stasio, *New York Times Book Review*

"Westlake knows precisely how to grab a reader, draw him or her into the story, and then slowly tighten his grip until escape is impossible."
—*Washington Post Book World*

"A pleasure . . . . Westlake's ability to construct an action story filled with unforeseen twists and quadruple-crosses is unparalleled."
—*San Francisco Chronicle*

"Donald Westlake's Parker novels are among the small number of books I read over and over. Forget all that crap you've been telling yourself about *War and Peace* and Proust—*these* are the books you'll want on that desert island."
—Lawrence Block

"To me, Richard Stark is the Prince of Noir."
—Martin Cruz Smith

"Gritty and chillingly noir . . . . [Westlake] succeeds in demonstrating his total mastery of crime fiction."
—*Booklist*

more . . .

PAYBACK

RICHARD STARK

WARNER BOOKS

A Time Warner Company

Mysterious Press Edition

Copyright © 1962 by Richard Stark
All rights reserved.

This Mysterious Press edition is published by arrangement with the author.

 Mysterious Press books are published by Warner Books, Inc., 1271 Avenue of the Americas, New York, NY 10020.

Visit our Web site at www.warnerbooks.com

A Time Warner Company

The Mysterious Press name and logo are registered trademarks of Warner Books, Inc.

Printed in the United States of America

First Mysterious Press Printing: March 1999

10 9 8 7 6 5 4 3 2 1

Library of Congress Cataloging-in-Publication Data

Stark, Richard.
    Payback / Richard Stark.
        p.   cm.
  ISBN 978-0-446-67464-5
    I. Title.
    PS3573.E9P39   1998
    813'.54—dc21   98-5298
                                                                        CIP

Book design by Charles Sutherland

PAYBACK

Richard Stark
introduced by
Donald E. Westlake

Stephen King phoned me one day a few years ago. "I want the other half of your pen name," he said. "Okay," I said. And so the pseudonym come to murderous life in the King novel *The Dark Half* was named George Stark. I don't know where the George came from.

Earlier, Stephen had made off with the front half of my pen name. He was using a pseudonym himself for the first time, and at the particular moment that his agent called to ask what the new name would be, he was reading a Richard Stark novel and listening to Bachman-Turner Overdrive, so that's how Richard Bachman was born.

Well, what the heck, I wasn't being Richard Stark any more; why not let him have an outing? On the other hand, when I did the screenplay from Jim Thompson's novel *The Grifters,* the movie's director, Stephen Frears, insisted it was Richard Stark who had written it, and even pressed me to use Richard Stark as the name in the credits. I got out of that one by explaining Richard Stark wasn't a member of the Writers Guild.

I don't think he's a joiner, actually.

The names we don't get from our parents can come from anywhere. I used *Richard* because I was thinking of Richard Widmark, in his first movie, *Kiss of Death,* in which part of the character's fascination and danger is in his unpredictability. He's fast and mean, and that's what I wanted the writing to be: crisp and lean, no fat, trimmed down . . . *stark.*

I needed a pen name just then because I'd decided to do something different. At that time, I was writing more or less normal whodunits, published in hardcover by Random House, under my own name, and I wanted to try something more hardboiled and rough-edged, troublesome in the manner of some people I'd known, and aimed at paperback publication. Aimed specifically, as a matter of fact, at Gold Medal Books, which published the cream of such writing at that time.

So I did a book without a hero, centering on the bad guy, paying attention to what *he* wanted and how he went about getting it, and where it led him. I wanted to start him with nothing except a desire for revenge, and let him construct himself. And at the end of the novel, because I knew what was supposed to happen at the end of tough guy novels, my lead character got caught by the police.

I never saw that book as the start of a series, never thought the bad guy could get off scot-free to come back and be a bad guy some more. If I'd known what was going to happen, I might have given him a first name, and he most likely wouldn't have been called Parker. Why not? Well, he was in a lot of automobiles over the course of sixteen books, and it got tiresome, after a while, trying to find some other way to say, "Parker parked the car."

In any event, I'd written a simple revenge story with a nonhero in the lead, who gets his comeuppance at the end, and I was going to sell it to Gold Medal Books, and then I'd go off and write something else, and maybe some day Richard Stark would come back and do a second novel, about some other character entirely. And the first thing that happened was that Gold Medal rejected the book, and the second thing that happened was that a brilliant editor and wonderful man named Bucklin Moon, at Pocket Books, read the manuscript and phoned me to say, "I'm considering buying this. Is there any way that Parker could escape from the police at the end, and you could give me three books a year about him?"

Well, yes. It turned out, Parker was a very interesting character to follow. I followed him for fourteen years, over sixteen books, and then, just in the same way that he'd so easily escaped from those cops at the end of the first novel (once I'd given him his head), he suddenly and just as easily escaped from me. Or from Richard Stark. Or maybe it was Richard Stark who'd escaped. Whatever the mechanics, after twelve years of dual personality, I was suddenly alone.

I tried not to be. Three times over the next ten years I tried to tell another Parker story, and he just refused to show up. I could write sentences, but they didn't refer to that guy, and they weren't the kind of sentences Richard Stark would write. So the hell with it, I could do other things.

Then came *The Grifters,* about which, in an odd way, Stephen Frears was right. That *was* Richard Stark, rousing himself from whatever. And just as I started work on the script, along came a five-month-long Writers Guild strike. Couldn't do film work, so I started *another* story about Parker, and it too turned into a dry well, just as the strike ended. Never again, says I.

Until, two years ago, my wife, Abby, suggested I look again at that last fragment, which I did, and saw it had life in it after all. I showed it to a friend, Otto Penzler, of the Mysterious Bookshop in New York, and said, "Is this Stark, or is this me imitating Stark?" He assured me it was Stark. He was back!

The book came into existence then as easily as all the others had done, and was called, had to be called, *Comeback*. Parker had years of stories waiting to be told, so now I have another new one, *Backflash*, and I'm working on the next, *Flashfire*.

Somehow, it must simply have been that the time was right for Richard Stark. Between the writing of *Comeback* and *Backflash*, a man named Brian Helgeland, co-screenwriter (and Academy Award recipient) for *L.A. Confidential*, wrote and directed, with Mel Gibson, a movie, *Payback*, based on *The Hunter*, that very first Richard Stark novel. (*The Hunter* had also been filmed in 1967, as *Point Blank*, with Lee Marvin, so the new one is technically a remake of the old one, but Helgeland based his script on the original novel.)

In 1961, when I wrote about Parker for the first time, I had no idea he would ever appear in another book. I had no idea he and his creator, Richard Stark, would become for a while, around 1970, better known and better paid than I was. I had no idea Parker would appear in (so far) seven movies. I also had no idea he would just up one day and disappear. And I certainly had no idea he would ever come back, and be welcomed all over again. (I'm sorry to do this to Stephen King, of course, but I think he'll survive the blow.)

Well, here's Richard Stark again, as he began. Now we are once again two, and we are both pleased.

ONE

1

When a fresh-faced guy in a Chevy offered him a lift, Parker told him to go to hell. The guy said, "Screw you, buddy," yanked his Chevy back into the stream of traffic, and roared on down to the tollbooths. Parker spat in the right-hand lane, lit his last cigarette, and walked across the George Washington Bridge.

The 8 A.M. traffic went *mmmmmm, mmmmmm,* all on this side, headed for the city. Over there, lanes and lanes of nobody going to Jersey. Underneath, the same thing.

Out in the middle, the bridge trembled and swayed in the wind. It does it all the time, but he'd never noticed it. He'd never walked it before. He felt it shivering under his feet, and he got mad. He threw the used-up butt at the river, spat on a passing hubcap, and strode on.

Office women in passing cars looked at him and felt vibrations above their nylons. He was big and shaggy, with flat square shoulders and arms too long in sleeves too short. He wore a gray suit, limp with age and no pressing. His shoes and socks were both black and both holey. The shoes were holey on the bottom, the socks were holey at heel and toe.

His hands, swinging curve-fingered at his sides, looked like they were molded of brown clay by a sculptor who thought big and liked veins. His hair was brown and dry and dead, blowing around his head like a poor toupee about to fly loose. His face was a chipped chunk of concrete, with eyes of flawed onyx. His mouth was a quick stroke, bloodless. His suit coat fluttered behind him, and his arms swung easily as he walked.

The office women looked at him and shivered. They knew he was a bastard, they knew his big hands were born to slap with, they knew his face would never break into a smile when he looked at a woman. They knew what he was, they thanked God for their husbands, and still they shivered. Because they knew how he would fall on a woman in the night. Like a tree.

The office men drove by, clutching their steering wheels, and hardly noticed him. Just a bum walking on the bridge. Didn't even own a car. A few of them saw him and remembered themselves before they'd made it when *they* didn't have a car. They thought they were empathizing with him. They thought it was the same thing.

Parker walked across the bridge and turned right. He went down that way one block to the subway hole. All down the street ahead of him were the blacktop and the sidewalks and the gray apartment buildings and the traffic lights at every intersection going from red to green to red. And lots of people, on the move.

He trotted down the steps into the subway hole. The spring sun disappeared, and there were fluorescent lights against cream-shaded tile. He went over to the subway-system map and

stood in front of it, scratching his elbow and not looking at the
map. He knew where he wanted to go.

The downtown train pulled in, already crowded, and the
doors slid back. More people pushed on. Parker turned, yanked
open the NO ADMITTANCE door and went on through. Somebody
behind him shouted, "Hey!" Ahead, the subway doors slid at
each other. He jumped, ran into the people standing in the car,
and the doors met behind him.

He went all the way downtown, got out at Chambers and
walked over to the Motor Vehicle Bureau on Worth. On the way,
he panhandled a dime from a latent fag with big hips and
stopped in a grimy diner for coffee. He bummed a cigarette from
the counter girl. It was a Marlboro. He twisted off the filter,
threw it on the floor, and stuck the cigarette between his bloodless lips. She lit it for him, leaning over the counter toward him
with her breasts high, like an offering. He got the cigarette
fired, nodded, dropped the dime on the counter, and went out
without a word.

She looked after him, face red with rage, and threw his dime
into the garbage. Half an hour later, when the other girl said
something to her, she called her a bitch.

Parker went on to the Motor Vehicle Bureau and stood at the
long wooden table while he filled out a driver's license form with
one of the old-fashioned straight pens. He blotted the form,
folded it carefully, and stuck it into his wallet, which was brown
leather and completely empty and beat to hell.

He left the Bureau and walked over to the post office, where
the federal government was in charge and they had ball-point
pens. He took out the license and stood hunched over it, sketch-
ing with small quick strokes in the space reserved for the state

stamp. The ball-point pen had ink of almost the right color, and Parker's memory of the stamp was clear.

When he was finished, it looked all right for anybody who didn't inspect it closely. It just looked as though the rubber stamp hadn't been inked well enough or had been jiggled when it was pressed to the paper or something. He smudged the damp ink a bit more with his finger, licked the finger clean, and returned the license to his wallet. Then he crumpled and bent the wallet in his hands before putting it back in his hip pocket.

He walked up to Canal Street and went into a bar. It was dark in there, and clammy. The barman and his one customer stopped mumbling down at the end of the bar and looked at him, their expressions like those of fish looking out through the glass wall of a tank.

He went on down, ignoring them, and pushed open the spring door to the men's room. It slammed behind him.

He washed his face and hands in cold water without soap, because there wasn't any hot water and there wasn't any soap. He got his hair wet and pushed it around with his fingers until it looked all right. He stroked his palm up his jawline and felt the stubble, but it didn't show bad yet.

Taking his tie from his inside jacket pocket, he ran it taut through his fingers, to get the wrinkles out of it, and put it on. The wrinkles still showed. He had a safety pin attached to the lining of his jacket. He took it and pinned the tie to the shirt, where it wouldn't show. Pulled down that way, and with the jacket closed, it looked pretty good. And you couldn't see that the shirt was dirty any more.

He wet his fingers at the sink again, and forced the approximation of a crease into his pant legs, stroking down again and again until a vague line showed and stayed there. Then he looked at himself in the mirror.

He didn't look like any Rockefeller, but he didn't look like a bum either. He looked like a hard worker who never got out of the mailroom. Good enough. It would have to do.

He got out the driver's license one last time and dropped it on the floor. He squatted beside it, and patted the license here and there on the floor till it was reasonably dirty. Then he crumpled it some more, brushed the excess dirt off, and put it back in his wallet. One last rinsing of his hands, and he was ready to leave.

The bartender and his customer stopped mumbling again as he went by, but he didn't notice. He went back out into the sunlight and headed uptown and west, looking for just the right bank. He needed a bank that would have a lot of customers of the type he was faking.

When he found the one he wanted, he paused for a second and concentrated on rearranging his face. He stopped looking mean and he stopped looking mad. He kept working at it, and when he was sure he looked worried he went on into the bank.

There were four desks to his left, two of them occupied by middle-aged men in business suits. One of them was talking with an old woman in a cloth coat who was having trouble with English. Parker went straight over to the other and added a smile to the worried expression.

"Hello," he said, making his voice softer than usual. "I got a problem, and maybe you can help me. I've lost my checkbook, and I can't remember my account number."

"No problem at all," said the man, with a professional smile. "If you'll just give me your name. . . ."

"Edward Johnson," said Parker, giving him the name he'd put

on the license. He hauled his wallet out. "I've got identification. Here." He handed over the license.

The man looked at it, nodded, handed it back. "Fine," he said. "That was a special account?"

"That's right."

"One minute, please." He picked up his phone, talked into it for a minute, and waited, smiling reassurance at Parker. Then he talked a few seconds more and looked puzzled. He capped the phone mouthpiece with his hand and said to Parker, "There's no record of your account here. Are you *sure* it's a special account? No minimum balance?"

"Try the other kind," said Parker.

The man continued to look puzzled. He talked into the phone a while longer, then hung up, frowning. "There's no record of any account at all under that name."

Parker got to his feet. He grinned and shrugged. "Easy come, easy go," he said.

He walked out, and the man at the desk kept staring after him, frowning.

In the fourth bank he tried, Edward Johnson had a special checking account. Parker got the account number and the present balance, and a new checkbook to replace the one he'd lost. Edward Johnson only had six hundred dollars and change in his account. Parker felt sorry for him.

He left the bank, went into a men's clothing store, and bought a suit and a shirt and a tie and socks and shoes. He paid by check. The clerk compared the signature with the one on his driver's license, and called the bank to see if he had enough cash in his account to cover the check. He did.

He carried the packages up to the bus terminal on 40th

Street, and went up to the men's room. He didn't have a dime to open a stall door, so he crawled under it, pushing his packages ahead of him. He changed into the new clothes, transferred his wallet and checkbook, and left all the old clothes in the stall.

He walked north till he came to a leather goods shop. He bought a hundred and fifty dollars' worth of good luggage, a matched set of four pieces. He showed the driver's license for identification, and they didn't even call the bank. Two blocks he carried the luggage, and then he got thirty-five dollars for it at a pawn shop. He went crosstown, and did it twice more—luggage to pawn shop—and got another eighty dollars.

He took a cab up to 96th Street and Broadway, and worked up and down Broadway for a while, this time buying watches and pawning them. Then he went to Lexington Avenue, midtown, and did it some more. Four times all told, somebody called the bank to see if he had enough money in his account. Not once was his driver's license questioned as valid identification.

By three o'clock, he had a little over eight hundred dollars. He used one more check, to buy a medium-sized suitcase of excellent quality, and then he spent half an hour shopping, paying cash for his purchases. He bought a razor and lather and lotion, a toothbrush and paste, socks and underwear, two white shirts, three ties, a carton of cigarettes, a pint of hundred-proof vodka, a comb and brush set, and a new wallet. Everything except the wallet went into the suitcase.

When the suitcase was full, he quit shopping and went to a good restaurant for a steak. He undertipped, and ignored the waiter's dirty look as he went out, still carrying the suitcase. He took a cab to a medium-priced hotel, where they believed his driver's license and didn't make him pay in advance. He got a room and bath, and overtipped the bellboy.

He stripped out of the new clothes and took a bath. His body was hard and rangy and scarred. After the bath, he sat up naked in bed and slowly drank the pint of vodka straight from the bottle, grinning at the far wall. When the bottle was empty, he threw it at the wastebasket and fell asleep.

2

Parker closed the door behind him, and waited for the girl to get up off the floor. She looked up at him and her face went very white, and against the whiteness flared the ugly red mark where he had hit her.

She breathed his name and he said, "Get up. Cover yourself." He sounded disgusted. She didn't have anything on under the blue robe, and when she'd fallen the robe had dropped open below the waist. Her belly was white, but her legs were golden brown.

"You'll kill me," she said. There was no strength in her voice at all. It had the dull echoless quality of hopeless fear.

"Maybe not," he said. "Get up. Make coffee." He kicked her ankle gently. "Move it."

She slid backward along the floor, then rolled half over, her blond hair falling into her face, and struggled shakily to her feet.

At one point, she was bent far over, her back to him, palms and knees on the floor. He looked at her, and felt a sudden physical desire, like a knife twisting low in his abdomen. He leaned forward and smacked her backside instead. It didn't help.

He watched her. She straightened, keeping her back to him, and adjusted the robe, then walked through the apartment to the kitchen. He followed her.

It was an expensive apartment in an expensive building on an expensive block in the East Sixties. Inside the front door was a foyer, with a mirror and a table and a closet and an oriental rug. To the left, two steps led down between potted plants to the living room. More plants were spotted along the walls. There was other furniture, but the room was dominated by a long black coffee table and a longer white sofa.

In the right-hand wall, glass-paned double doors led to a dining room. Of the very few dining rooms left in Manhattan, this was one of the last. It was done like a traditional dining room, with the warm, wood table and chairs, the side tables, the glass-doored shelving lined with tumblers and brandy snifters and pilsner glasses, even the yellow-bulbed chandelier hanging over the table.

Another right turn from the dining room led to the kitchen. There was a swinging door. The girl pushed through it, and Parker followed her. He sat down at the table and looked up at the white-faced black-fingered clock on the white wall. Nearly five-thirty. The kitchen window showed black, but dawn wasn't too far away.

The girl opened a cupboard door and took down an electric coffee maker. She had to hunt around for the cord. Her face was expressionless, her movements neither slow nor fast, but she carefully kept from looking at him, and when she found the cord she dropped it on the floor.

Stooping to pick it up, she exposed her breasts to him. They were pale, like her belly, full, red tipped, soft looking. She didn't even know she'd done it. She was afraid for her life. She wasn't thinking about her body at all.

While the coffee was making, she stood gazing unseeing at the pot. He had to tell her when it was ready.

She got him a cup. He said, "Get two." She did, and poured them coffee, and sat down across from him not looking at him.

"Lynn," he said. His voice was harsh, but soft.

She raised her eyes, as though they were being hauled up by pulleys. She looked at him. "I had to," she whispered.

He said, "Where's Mal?"

She shook her head. "Gone. Moved out."

"Where?"

"I don't know. Honest to God."

"When?"

"Three months ago."

He sipped at the coffee. It was stronger than he liked, but that was all right. He shouldn't have come here.

Four in the morning, at the hotel, all of a sudden he'd been awake. And with the vodka still strong in him. So he'd come straight here.

It was just as well Mal was gone. When he met up with Mal, he didn't want any vodka in him.

He lit a cigarette, drank more coffee. He said, "Who pays the rent?"

"Mal," she said.

He got to his feet without a word, stepped swiftly through the swinging door to the dining room. He looked to the left, through the glass doors into the living room, then moved to his right, and shoved open the other door. He reached quickly in and switched on the light.

The bedroom was empty. He strode across and checked the bathroom, and it was empty, too.

Back in the bedroom, he noticed Lynn standing in the doorway, looking at him. He opened the closet. Dresses and skirts and blouses and sweaters. Women's shoes on the floor. He went over to the dresser, looked quickly through the drawers. Only female things.

He shook his head. He looked at her, still watching him from the doorway. "You live alone?"

She nodded.

"And Mal pays the rent?"

"Yes."

"All right. Let's go back to the kitchen."

Again, she led the way. He switched off the bedroom light and followed.

They finished their coffee in silence, and then he said, "Why?"

She jumped, startled, as shaken up as if a firecracker had gone off next to her ear. She gaped at him, and slowly her eyes focused, and she said, "What? I don't—I don't know what you mean."

He waved a hand, impatiently. "The rent," he said.

"Oh." She nodded, and brought her hands up to her face. They stayed there a few seconds, and then she inhaled shudderingly and lowered her hands again. Her face was no longer expressionless. Now it was ravaged. It was as though invisible weights were sewn to her cheeks, dragging the whole face down. "A payoff, I guess," she said. Her tone was hopeless, like before.

"Yeah," he said. He sounded mad again. He flipped his cigarette across the room into the sink. It sputtered, and he lit another one.

She said, "I'm glad you aren't dead. Isn't that stupid?"

"Yes."

She nodded. "You hate me. You got a right."

"I ought to slash you," he told her. "I ought to slash your nostrils. I ought to make you look like a witch, like the witch you are."

"You ought to kill me," she said hopelessly.

"Maybe I will."

Her head sagged down toward her chest. Her voice was almost inaudible. "I keep taking pills," she murmured. "Every night. If I don't take the pills, I don't sleep. I think about you."

"And how I'm coming for you?"

"No, and how you're dead. And I wish it was me."

"Take too many pills," he suggested.

"I can't. I'm a coward." She raised her head and looked at him again. "That's why I did it, Parker," she said. "I'm a coward. It was you dead, or me dead."

"And Mal pays the rent."

"I'm a coward," she said.

"Yeah. I know about that."

"I never gave him satisfaction, Parker. I never responded, no matter what he did."

"That why he moved out?"

"I think so."

He grinned, mirthlessly. "You can turn it on and off," he said bitterly. "A bed machine. None of it means a thing."

"Only with you, Parker."

He spat out a word like a slap. She recoiled from it, shaking her head. "It's the truth, Parker," she said. "That's why I need the pills. That's why I didn't quit this place and find some other guy. Mal keeps me going and he doesn't ask anything I can't give."

The coffee was replacing the vodka. He laughed, slapping the table, and said, "Good thing the bastard wasn't here, huh? I come barging in, he'd have two, three guys in the living room, huh? All the time, just in case."

She nodded. "He never stayed here alone."

"He's worried, the bastard." He nodded. He beat out a drumroll on the table edge with the first two fingers of each hand. "He thinks maybe I'll come back from the grave," he said. He laughed, and finished the drumroll with a rhythmic double crash of both hands on the table. "He's right, huh? Yeah. Back from the grave."

"What are you going to do, Parker?" she asked, and the quaver of fear had finally reached her voice.

"I'm going to drink his blood," he said. "I'm going to chew up his heart and spit it into the gutter for the dogs to raise a leg at. I'm going to peel the skin off him and rip out his veins and hang him with them." He sat in the chair, his fists clenching and unclenching, his eyes glaring at her. He snatched up the coffee cup and hurled it. It caromed off the refrigerator and shattered on the edge of the sink, then sprayed onto the floor.

She stared at him, mouth moving, but no sound coming out.

He looked at her, and his eyes hardened again to onyx. One side of his mouth grinned, and he said, "To you? You mean to you? What am I going to do to you?"

She didn't move.

"I don't know yet," he said. His voice was high and hard, like a tightrope walker out on the rope, knowing his balance was never better. High and hard and sharp. "It depends. It depends on you. Where's Mal?"

"Oh, Jesus," she whispered.

"It depends on you," he said again.

She shook her head. "I don't know, Parker. I swear on the Cross. I haven't seen him for three months. I don't even know if he's in New York."

"How do you get your payoff?"

"Messenger," she said. "The first of every month. He brings me an envelope, with cash in it."

"How much cash?"

"A thousand."

He smacked the table with stiff fingers. "Twelve grand a year. Tax free. The setup pays well, Lynn. The Judas ewe." He laughed harshly, like a knife slashing through canvas. "The Judas ewe," he repeated. "Wiggling her tail down the chute."

"I was *afraid!* They would have killed me, Parker. They would have hurt me and then they would have killed me."

"Yeah. Who is this messenger?"

"It's a different one each time. I don't know any of them."

"Sure," he said. "Mal don't trust you. Nobody trusts the Judas ewe."

"I didn't *want* to, Parker, I swear before all the saints! You were the only man I ever wanted. The only man I ever needed. But I had to."

"You'd do it again," he said.

She shook her head. "Not this time—not now. I couldn't go through this again."

"You're afraid to die," he said. He held his hands out and flexed them, looking at her throat.

She shrank away. "Yes. Yes, I'm afraid. I'm afraid to live, too. I couldn't go through it all over again."

"The first of the month," he said, "you'll open your mouth to the messenger. You'll say, 'Tell Mal to look out. Tell him Parker's in town.'"

She shook her head violently. "I've got no reason," she said desperately. "I'm going down to the core now, Parker. I'm telling you the bottom truth. If I had to, I would. I'd do it all over again, everything, if I had to. But I don't have to. Nobody knows you're here. Nobody knows you're alive. Nobody's threatening me, making me turn you up."

"Maybe you'll play it safe and volunteer," he said.

"No. That's no way to play it safe."

He laughed. "You been in the Army too? Or just nearby?"

Surprisingly, she flushed, and her answer was sullen. "I was never a whore, Parker," she said. "You know that."

"No. You sold my body instead."

He got to his feet and left the kitchen. She trailed after him, and he went into the living room. He stood for a minute glowering at the furniture, and then he sprawled on the sofa.

"I'll take a chance," he said. "I'll take a small chance. Mal can't trust you, so he didn't leave you any contacts. No phone numbers, no drops, nothing. So you can't play Judas ewe till the first of the month, when the messenger comes. Four days from now, when the messenger comes. Right?"

"Not then, either," she said, face and voice urgent. "I wouldn't, Parker—there's nobody forcing me."

He laughed again. "You won't get the chance," he said. "You

won't have to make the choice." He got up with a suddenness that terrified her, but he made no move toward her. "I'll meet him for you."

"Are you going to stay?" she asked him. Fear and desire were mixed up together in her expression. "Will you stay?"

"I'll stay."

He turned away from her, crossed the living room and pushed into the bedroom again. She followed, the tip of her tongue trembling between her lips, her eyes darting from him to the bed.

He circled the bed, knelt beside it, in front of the nightstand. He reached in under the nightstand and ripped the telephone wires loose. Then he straightened again.

She had opened her robe. He looked at her, and the desire stabbed him once more, stronger than the last time. He remembered her now.

She said, "Will you stay in here?"

He shook his head. "For you, that tree is dead."

He went over to the window, pushed the drapes aside and looked out. There was no fire escape, and no ledge.

She whispered his name.

He crossed the room again, headed toward the door. She took a step toward him, her arms coming up. He stepped around her, and went on to the door.

The key was in the lock on the inside. He took it out, stepped through the doorway, closed and locked the door.

On the other side, she called his name, just once.

He switched out the living room and kitchen lights, and lay down on the sofa. In the dark, he stared at the window. He had lied. The tree wasn't dead: he was afraid of her.

3

She was a corpse naked on the bed. He stood in the doorway a minute, looking at her. The drapes were drawn against the noon sun, leaving the room as cool and dark as a funeral parlor. An odor of perfume and cosmetics and cologne was vaguely flower-like. Where a faint breeze rippled the separation of the drapes, sunlight flickered like a candle flame. Far away there was the hum of traffic.

She lay on her back, breasts and belly flattened. She had apparently composed herself for death, legs together, hands crossed at the waist, elbows close to her sides. But, in falling asleep, she had moved, destroying the symmetry.

One knee had bent, the right leg now lying awkwardly L-shaped, the wrinkled sole of her right foot against the side of the left knee, in a kind of graceless parody of ballet. Her left hand was still reposed, palm down, over her navel, but her right arm had fallen away and lay now outstretched, palm up and fingers curled. Her head was canted at an angle to the right, and her mouth had fallen open.

Parker came into the room, strode around the bed, and picked up the empty pill bottle from the nightstand. Printed on the label was the name and address and phone number of the drug store. Typed in the white space below were Lynn's name, the name of a doctor, a number, and the message: "One on retiring as necessary. Do not exceed dosage."

Parker moved his lips as he read.

He read the whole thing twice, the name of the drug store and the address and the phone number and his dead wife's name and the name of the doctor and the number and the message. Then he dropped the pill bottle into the half-full wastebasket beside the nightstand, and turned to look at the corpse again.

He moved as though to touch her wrist, to feel for a pulse, but then he checked the motion. A corpse is a corpse; there can be no mistake. The skin is too waxlike, the chest too still, the lips too dry, the eyes too sunken behind the closed lids.

He had to get rid of her. He had three days to stay here, and she couldn't be here with him. In all his rages, six months on the prison farm, he had never planned to kill her. To beat her, yes, to mutilate her, to give her pain and scars, but not to see her dead.

In the closet, he found a dress with a zipper all the way down the back. He put it on her, forcing her stiffening arms through the sleeves, then rolled her over and zipped it closed and rolled her back again. He forced shoes onto her feet. They were too small. Either the feet had started to swell or she had gone in for shoes more flattering than comfortable.

Dressed, she looked less dead. Not asleep, though. Unconscious. As though she'd been clipped. He closed her mouth, and it stayed closed.

At the doorway, he looked at her for a long minute. Then he said, "You were always dumb. You never changed."

He shut the door.

There was a television set in the living room. He found a bottle of blended whiskey in a kitchen cupboard, broke the seal, and watched cartoons on television. Then he watched situation comedy reruns and children's shows.

The living room drapes were closed, but he could tell by the clock over the television set when the sun was going down. He watched dinner-hour news broadcasts, and they didn't mention him. They wouldn't. The break was three weeks ago. A continent ago. A dead guard and a runaway vag don't make the news a continent away.

It should never have happened. Another result of her dumbness. Sixty days as a vag, and now they had his prints on file, the marks of his fingers. The name that went with the marks was Ronald Casper, but it didn't matter. He could call himself anything, even his true name, and the marks of his fingers would never change. Sixty days they gave him. Twenty days, and he fought a guard, and they added six more months. Eight months out of his life, weeding on the prison farm. He lasted six and found his break, and took it—and left behind a stupid guard with his head half twisted from his shoulders.

She had caused that, just one of the things she'd done to him. Crossed him and cuckolded him and jailed him and put his prints on file in Washington, D.C. Given him a continent to cross. *She* had done it.

No other woman could have. There had never been a woman anywhere in the world to trouble him, till her. There never would be again.

And now she had left him a body to dispose of. He couldn't leave her here, he had a messenger to meet. He couldn't keep her here, he wouldn't be able to stand that. He couldn't call for the law to come take her away, like a solid citizen, because one hard look would tell them he wasn't a solid citizen.

He hated her. He hated her and he loved her, and he'd never felt either emotion for anyone before. Never love, never hate, never for anyone. Mal, now. Mal he would kill, but that wasn't hate. There was a score to settle; there were accounts to balance. That was rage, that was fury and pride, but it wasn't hate.

The level lowered in the whiskey bottle, and the prime-time panel shows and westerns came on the television set. He sat and watched, the blue-white light gleaming on his face, outlining the ridges of his cheekbones. Prime time went by, and the old movies started, and he watched them. The movies finished, and a minister said a prayer, and a choir sang the "Star-Spangled Banner" while a flag fluttered on the screen, and then the station went off the air. The speaker emitted only a heavy hissing; the screen was full of a trembling of black and white spots.

He roused himself, switched the set off, turned on lights. The bottle was empty. He felt a little high, and that was bad. That was something else she'd done, made him drink himself a little high when he shouldn't.

He went out to the kitchen and made a sandwich, and washed it down with half a quart of milk. He was tired then, so he made coffee and drank three cups black, and doused his face at the kitchen sink.

The bedroom was dark. Light spilled in from the living room, across her shod feet. He switched on the ceiling light, and she had moved. Her arms and legs had twisted in toward her torso;

her head was back, her eyes were open and staring at the closed drapes.

He pushed down the eyelids, and they stayed down. Her limbs resisted when he straightened them out. He picked her up, like a groom about to carry his bride across the threshold, and bore her out of the bedroom, across the living room to the front door.

The hall was empty. He pushed the button and the elevator came up from the first floor. He took it down to the basement, carrying her, and found the back way out of the building.

An alley took him to the street a block from the front of her building. He turned right and walked down the half-block to Fifth Avenue and Central Park. On the way, a man passed him, hurrying by, giving him scarcely a look. At the corner, a cruising cab sidled close, the driver leaning over to call out, "You want a cab, mister?"

"We live just down the block."

The cabby grinned. "Got a load on, huh?"

"She isn't used to vodka," he said.

The cab cruised on. There were no pedestrians. He waited for a Jaguar sedan to pass, going uptown, and the couple in it glanced at him and grinned and looked away. He crossed the street and stepped over the low stone wall into the park.

In a blackness of shrubbery, he laid her down. Working by feel, unable to see what he was doing, he stripped off the dress and the shoes again. He took out his pen knife. Holding her jaw in his left hand to guide him in the darkness, he stroked the knife across her face. Otherwise, the law would try to have her identified by running a photo in the papers. Mal would read the papers.

There was no blood on his hands, very little on the knife. A corpse doesn't bleed much. He wiped the knife on the dress, closed it, put it back in his pocket. He rolled the shoes in the dress, tucked the bundle under his left arm and walked out of the park and back to the apartment.

He was very tired now, and he was moving unsteadily by the time he entered the apartment. He switched off all the lights and stretched out on the couch. He fell asleep at once.

4

Three days of no sound but what droned from the television set. The apartment smelled stale, as though she were still in it. He didn't wait well.

There was a calendar on the kitchen wall, with a photograph of two cocker spaniels in front of a rose bush. He spent a lot of time looking at the dates, sitting at the kitchen table with a coffee cup in his hand.

The third day began the new month. Parker roamed the living room, drawn constantly to the front door. He would spend five minutes at a time standing in front of the door, listening, waiting for the sound of the bell. Twice he reached out and touched the knob, but he didn't open the door.

There were still two bottles of whiskey in the cupboard, but he didn't touch them. She wouldn't do that to him, not again. She had troubled him for the last time.

As it turned out, he was making fresh coffee when the bell rang. He stopped, holding the spoon, head raised, and turned toward the sound. Then he finished what he was doing and went through the apartment to the front door. He opened the peep-hole and studied the face of the messenger. He had never seen it before.

The messenger was a short butterball and a cracked fashion plate. He wore a narrow-lapeled suit of a bright garish blue that had never been in style, and only the middle button of the coat was fastened. His shirt was the harsh white of snow in sunlight and at the collar was a multi-colored bow tie. The shirt seemed to be starched; not just the collar, the whole shirt.

The face above this elegance was chubby and cheerful. The eyes were blue and small, set wide apart in fat. An inane half-smile curved the lips. The ears were pink and large and soft. And atop the head perched a straw hat, at a jaunty angle.

The messenger's suitcoat was so tight Parker could see the outline of the money envelope in the inside pocket. Mal must be sure of himself to send a thing like this.

Parker opened the door. The butterball blinked at him, and the half-smile faded. A delicate frown puckered the brows, and he said in a tiny high voice, "Do I have the wrong apartment? I must, I must have the wrong apartment."

"You want Lynn Parker?"

"Yes. Yes." The butterball bent at the waist, peering past Parker. "Is she here?"

"Come on in," said Parker.

"No, no. I must not. Is she here?"

Parker reached out and clutched a handful of shirtfront. He pulled, and the butterball stumbled inside, eyes and mouth wide open, hands splayed out in front of him as though he'd fall. Parker looked out into the hall, saw that it was empty, and came back inside, slamming the door.

The butterball was recovering his balance, and Parker shoved him again, sending him reeling into the living room. One way or another he managed not to land on his face.

Parker followed him into the living room, noticing details he hadn't been able to see through the peephole, like the shoes, which were a light russet tan with perforated curlicues over the toe. And between the top of the shoes and the cuffless bottom of the trouser legs there was at least an inch of space, occupied by canary yellow socks.

The butterball stood all aquiver in the middle of the living room. His hands were pressed to his chest, fingers spread, either to protect himself or the envelope he was supposed to deliver.

Parker held his hand out. "Give me the dough."

"I must not! I must, I must see Miss Parker."

"I'm her husband."

The fact meant nothing to the butterball, that was obvious. "I was told—they told me only to see Miss Parker."

"Who told you?" Parker asked.

"Where is Miss Parker? I must, I must see Miss Parker."

"I've taken over the route. Give me the dough."

"I must, I must telephone. May I telephone?" He peeked around the room, then his eyes flickered warily to Parker.

Parker stepped quickly over in front of him and yanked on the jacket lapel. The one button holding the jacket closed came off with a pop, and Parker took the bulky envelope out of the inside pocket. He tossed it at the armchair to his left.

The butterball fluttered his arms, crying, "You must not! You must not!"

Parker held his left hand rigid, fingers together and extended, and chopped the butterball in the midsection, just above the gold monogrammed belt buckle. The butterball opened his mouth, but neither sound nor air came out. In slow motion, his hands folded across his stomach, his knees buckled, and he fell forward into Parker's right fist. Then he hit the floor cold.

Parker emptied his pockets, searching every item. The wallet contained a driver's license, a library card, a numbers slip with 342 on it, and fourteen dollars. The license and library card agreed that the butterball was named Sidney Chalmers, and that he lived on West 92nd Street.

Another pocket produced seventy-three cents in change and a Zippo lighter with S.C. inscribed on its side in Gothic script. A slip of paper with Lynn's name and address on it was in the side pocket of the jacket. There was nothing anywhere to tell where he'd picked up the envelope for Lynn.

Parker left him sprawled on the carpet and went into the kitchen. A search of the drawers resulted in a roll of slender but strong twine. Going back to the living room, Parker lashed the butterball's wrists and ankles securely, then propped him up with his back against the sofa, his head lolling back on the cushion. Then Parker slapped him and pinched him till he groaned and squirmed and his eyelids fluttered open.

Parker straightened, standing tall and ominous, gazing deadpan down at the terrified butterball. "Tell me where Mal Resnick is."

The butterball licked trembling lips. "Hu-who?"

Parker bent, slapped him backhanded across the face, straightened, and repeated his question.

The butterball blinked like a metronome. His chin quivered. Fat tears squiggled down his cheeks. "I don't know," he pleaded. "I don't know who you mean."

"The guy who gave you the envelope."

"Oh, I must not!"

"Oh, you must," Parker mimicked. He put his right foot on the butterball's crossed, tied ankles, and gradually added weight. "You sure as hell must."

"Help!" sobbed the butterball. "Help! Help!"

Parker kicked him in the stomach. "Wrong words," he said. "Don't do that again." He waited till the butterball had air in his lungs again. "Give me his name."

"Please—they'll kill me."

"*I'll* kill you. Worry about me."

The butterball closed his eyes, and his whole face sagged in an expression of complete and comic despair. Parker waited, and at last the butterball said, without opening his eyes, "Mr. Stegman. Mr. Arthur Stegman."

"Where do I find him?"

"In—in Brooklyn. The Rockaway Car Rental. Farragut Road near Rockaway Parkway."

"Fine. You should have saved yourself some trouble."

"They'll kill me," he sobbed. "They'll kill me."

Parker went down on one knee, untied the twine around the butterball's ankles, straightened up and said, "Get to your feet."

He couldn't do it by himself; Parker had to help him.

The butterball stood weaving, breathing like a bellows. Parker turned him around, shoved him across the living room into the bedroom, tripped him up and sent him crashing to the floor. He tied his ankles again, then went out and locked the bedroom door behind him.

He gathered up the envelope full of money, slipped it into his jacket pocket, and left the apartment.

5

The subway line ended at Rockaway Parkway and Glenwood Road, in Canarsie. Parker asked directions of the old woman in the change booth. Farragut Road was one block to the right.

The Rockaway Car Rental was a small shack on a lot between two private houses. The lot was sandy and weed scraggled, with three elderly white-painted Checker cabs parked on it. The shack was small, of white clapboard, with a plate-glass window in front.

Inside, there was a railing around the guy at the two-way radio. A bedraggled sofa was along the other wall, and a closed door led to the room in back.

Parker leaned on the chest-high railing and said, "I'm looking for Arthur Stegman."

The radioman put down his *Daily News* and said, "He ain't here right now. Maybe I can help you."

"You can't. Where do I find him?"

"I'm not sure. If you'd leave your—"

"Take a guess."

"What?"

"About where he is. Take a guess."

The radioman frowned. "Now hold on a second, buddy. You want to—"

"Is he home?"

The radioman gnawed his cheek a few seconds, then said, "Why don't you go ask him?"

He picked up his *News* again.

"I'll be glad to," said Parker. "Where's he live?"

"We don't give that information out," said the radioman. He swiveled around in his chair and studied the *News*.

Parker tapped a thumbnail on the top of the railing. "You're making a mistake, employee," he said. "Sidney run off."

The radioman looked up and frowned. "What's that supposed to mean?"

"To you, maybe, nothing. To Stegman, plenty."

The radioman frowned harder, thinking it over. Then he shook his head. "No," he said. "If Art wanted to see you, he'd of told you where to find him."

"Right here," Parker said.

"For that, all you need is a phone book. No sale." He went back to his *News* again.

Parker shook his head angrily, and strode toward the door at the back of the room. Behind him, the radioman jumped up, shouting something, but Parker ignored him. He pushed open the door and walked in.

Six men were sitting around a round table, playing seven-card stud. They looked up, and Parker said, "I'm looking for Stegman."

A florid-faced guy with his hat jammed far back on his head said, "Who the hell invited you?"

The one in the police uniform said, "Get lost."

The radioman came in then, and said to the florid-faced guy, "He just won't take no for an answer." He reached for Parker. "Come on, bum. Enough is enough."

Parker knocked away the reaching hand, and brought up his knee. The radioman grunted and rested his brow on Parker's shoulder. Parker sidestepped, ignoring the radioman, who sagged in a half-crouch against the wall. "I'm still looking for Stegman."

The one in the police uniform threw down his cards and got to his feet. "That looks to me like assault," he said.

The florid-faced guy said, "Willy will sign the complaint, Ben. Don't you worry."

Another of the players, a tall hard-faced man in a white shirt and no tie, said, "This bird looks to me like the kind resists arrest. What do you think, Ben?"

"Maybe you ought to help me, Sal," the cop said.

Parker shook his head. "You don't want to play around. I got a message for Stegman."

"Hold it," said the florid-faced guy. Ben and Sal stopped where they were. "What's the message?"

"You Stegman?"

"I'll tell him when I see him."

"Yeah. You're Stegman, all right. I come to tell you Sidney's run off."

Stegman sat forward in his chair. "What?"

"You heard me. He run off with the thousand. He never even went to see the girl."

"You're crazy. Sidney wouldn't dare do—" He stopped, looked quickly at the other players, and got to his feet. "Deal me out. Come on, you, we'll talk outside."

"What about this assault?" the cop, Ben, said.

Stegman made an angry gesture. "The hell with that. Go on back to the game."

"What if Willy wants to sign a complaint?"

"He don't. Do you, Willy?"

Willy, upright now, but still ashen faced, said, "No. All I want's a return bout."

Stegman shook his head. "On your own time, Willy," he said. "Come on, you."

Parker followed him to the front office, where Stegman went behind the railing and took one of the keys from the rack on the wall. "I'm taking the Chrysler, Willy," he called into the back room. "I'm going down to the beach. Be gone twenty minutes."

"Twenty minutes. Okay." Willy came to the door and looked at Parker. "I'm on my own time startin' six o'clock," he said.

Parker turned his back and walked out the shack after Stegman. Stegman pointed at a black nine-passenger Chrysler limousine. "We'll take that. We can't talk in the office. No privacy. Those guys don't know nothin' about this stuff."

They got into the limousine, and Stegman drove it out around the shack to the street. Looking out the rear window, Parker saw the cop standing in the shack doorway, frowning.

Stegman drove up to the corner of Rockaway Parkway and turned left. "You can start talking any time," he said.

Parker pointed at the two-way radio under the dashboard. "If you're not back in twenty minutes, Sparks calls you, is that it?"

"And if I don't answer," Stegman answered, "he calls every other car I've got. How come you know about Sidney?"

"I was with the girl. Lynn Parker."

Stegman glanced at him, then back at the traffic. "You know a lot. How come I don't recognize you?"

"I just got in town. Watch your driving, there's a lot of kids."

"I know how to drive."

"Maybe we better wait till we get to this beach."

Stegman shrugged.

They drove nine blocks down Rockaway Parkway, then through an underpass under the Belt Parkway and around a circle to a broad cobblestone pier sticking out into Jamaica Bay. There were a couple of Parks Department–type buildings out at the far end of the pier. The rest was parking lot, with a few small skinny trees, the whole surrounded by a railed concrete walk and benches.

Stegman stopped in the parking lot, which was almost empty. "The Bay's polluted," he said. "There's no swimming here. Kids come here at night and neck, that's all." He shifted in the seat, facing Parker, and said, "Now what's this about Sidney? He wouldn't dare run off with the dough."

"He didn't." Parker took the envelope out of his pocket and dropped it on top of the dashboard. "I took it away from him."

Stegman's hand reached toward the radio switch. "What the hell is this? What are you up to?"

"Touch that switch and I'll break your arm."

Stegman's hand stopped.

Parker nodded. "I'm looking for Mal Resnick," he said. "You're going to tell me where he is."

"No. Even if I knew, the answer would still be no."

"You'll tell me. I want to tell him he doesn't have to pay her off any more."

"Why not?"

"She's dead. So is your fat pansy. You can be dead, too, if you want."

Stegman licked his lips. He turned his head and nodded at the small stone buildings out at the end of the pier. "There's people there," he said. "All I got to do is holler."

"You'd never get it out. Take a deep breath and you're dead. Open your mouth wide and you're dead."

Stegman looked back at him. "I don't see no gun," he said. "I don't see no weapon."

Parker held up his hands. "You see two of them," he said. "They're all I need."

"You're out of your mind. It's broad daylight. We're in the front seat of a car. People see us scuffling—"

"There wouldn't be any scuffle, Stegman. I'd touch you once, and you'd be dead. Look at me. You know this isn't a bluff."

Stegman met his eye, and Parker waited. Stegman blinked, and looked down at the radio. Parker said, "You don't have that long. He won't be calling for ten minutes. You'll be dead in five if you don't tell me where Mal is."

"I don't know where he is. That's the truth. I believe you— you're crazy enough to try it—but that's still the truth. I don't know where he is."

"You got that dough from him."

"There's a checking account in the bank near my office. On Rockaway Parkway. There's a hundred bucks in it to keep it alive. Every month Mal deposits eleven hundred. Then I write a check and take it out. I keep the hundred for myself and send the grand to the girl. A different messenger every month, the way he wanted it."

Parker gnawed on his cheek.

Stegman said, "He's scared of the girl. That's the way it looks to me."

"He must have left you a way to get in touch with him."

"No. He said he'd see me around." Stegman exhaled sharply, shaking his head. "Mister," he said, "I don't know nothing about this. I don't know who you are, or the girl, or why the payoff. Mal and I used to hang around together in the old days, before he went out to California. So he shows up three months ago and says do him a favor. I'll pick up an extra C a month, and there's no problem, no law, nothing. So I'll do him the favor, what the hell. But now you come around and talk about killing me. That much a buddy of Mal I'm not. If I knew where he was, I'd tell you. That's straight. If he was setting me up for this, some guy coming around going to kill me, he should have picked another boy. He should have told me what might happen. You think I'd come out for a ride with you?"

Parker shrugged. "All right."

"I'll tell you this much. He's in New York, that I know."

"How do you know?"

"He said so. When he come around for me to do this little favor. I asked him how he liked it out west, and he said he was through out there. From now on, he was staying in the big town. He got like lonesome, he said."

"So where would he be? You know him from the old days. Where would he hang out?"

"I don't have any idea. He was gone a long time."

"You could check."

"I could *say* I'd check. Then you'd get out of the car, and I'd mind my own business some more. And I'd tell my drivers, they see you around again, they should jump on you with both feet." He shrugged. "You know that as well as I do."

Parker nodded. "So I'll find him some other way. You want Sidney back, you send somebody up to Lynn Parker's place. I got him locked in the bedroom."

"I thought you said he was dead."

"He isn't."

"Is the girl there, too?"

"No. She's in the morgue. All right, let's go back. You can drop me off at the subway."

"Sure." Stegman stopped for a red light and shook his head. "This'll teach me. No more favors."

"You came out all right. So far."

Stegman turned his head. "What do you mean, so far?"

"You happen to run into Mal somewhere, you don't want to mention me."

"Don't worry, friend. No more favors!"

6

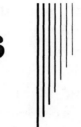

He changed trains three times, but there wasn't anyone following him. He was disgusted. It meant Stegman was telling the truth, and it was a dead end. Otherwise, a tail would have led to the connection.

He wanted Mal. He wanted Mal between his hands. . . .

It had started ten months ago. There were four of them in it: Parker and his wife and Mal and a Canadian hotshot named Chester. Chester was the one who set it up. He'd heard about the arms deal, and he saw the angle right away. He brought Mal into it, and Mal brought in Parker.

It was a sweet setup. Eighty thousand dollars' worth of munitions, with over-writes along the way bringing the total up to ninety-three grand and change. The goods were American, picked up here and there, and trucked piecemeal into Canada. It was easier to get the stuff into Canada than either into Mexico or out of a United States port, and once in Canada there was no trouble getting it airborne.

There was a small airfield up in Keewatin, near Angikuni

Lake, and at the right time of year the roads were passable. There were two planes, making two trips each, heading first westward over MacKenzie and Yukon and B.C. to the Pacific, and then turning south. One island stop for refueling, and then on southward again. The buyers were South American revolutionaries with a mountain airfield and a yen for bloodshed.

Chester learned about the transaction through a friend of his who'd gotten a job driving one of the trucks north into Canada. He learned the details of the operation and knew that, in a deal like this, payment would have to be in cash. That made it a natural for a hijacking. There would never be any law called in, and there was nothing to fear from a bunch of mountain guerrillas a continent away.

As to the Americans and Canadians doing the selling, they wouldn't care; they wouldn't be out of pocket at all. They'd still have their munitions, and there was always a market for munitions.

The truck driver didn't know when or where the money was supposed to change hands, but Chester found out from him the name of a man who did know, a lawyer named Bleak from San Francisco, one of the backers who'd put up the money in the states for the initial purchase of the arms. He also learned that he had five weeks before the arms would all have been delivered to the field in Keewatin.

Chester at that time was a straight busher when it came to operations like armed robbery. Most of his experience was with cross-the-border running of one kind or another. He'd bring pornography into the states and bootleg it in Chicago or Detroit, transport cigarettes north and whiskey south, wheel bent goods into Canada for sale fence-to-fence, and things like that.

He'd taken one fall, in a Michigan pen, when he was stopped at the border in a hot car with a bad daub job. The motor number was still there for all the world to see. And the spare tire was full of Chesterfields.

A small, thin, narrow-faced ferret of a man, Chester knew the munitions money was pie on the sill, but he was also smart enough to know he wasn't smart enough to take it away by himself. So he drifted south into Chicago, full of his information, and there hooked up with Mal Resnick.

Mal Resnick was a big-mouth coward who'd blown a syndicate connection four years before and was making a living these days in a hack, steering for some of the local business. The way he'd loused up with the syndicate, he lost his nerve and dumped forty thousand dollars of uncut snow he was delivering when he mistook the organization linebacker for a plainclothes cop. They took three of his teeth and kicked him out in the street, telling him to go earn the forty grand and then come back. He'd worked intermediary once or twice in the last year for Chester peddling pornography.

If Chester had a failing, it was that he believed people were what they thought they were. Mal Resnick, despite the syndicate error, still thought of himself as a redhot, a smart boy with guts and connections. Chester believed him, and so it was to Mal he went with the story of the munitions and the ninety-three thousand dollars. They discussed it over the table in Mal's roach-ridden kitchen, and Mal, seeing the potential as clearly as Chester had, immediately bought in.

The operation, at this point, ran into a snag that threatened to hold it up forever. Despite his promises and his big words, Mal didn't really know anybody worth adding to the group, but he couldn't bring himself to admit the fact to Chester. He stalled the little man off, while desperately looking up old syndicate acquaintances, with none of whom he'd ever been very close anyway, and all of whom were content with the work they had. They didn't even want to listen to his proposition. This went on for ten days, until the night Parker and his wife hailed Mal's cab just off the Loop.

Parker wasn't a syndicate boy, and never had been. He worked a job every year or so, payroll or armored car or bank, never taking anything but unmarked and untraceable cash. He never worked with more than four or five others, and never came in on a job unless he was sure of the competence of his associates. Nor did he always work with the same people.

He kept his money in hotel safes, and lived his life in resort hotels—Miami, Las Vegas and Palm Springs—taking on another job only when his cash on hand dropped below five thousand dollars. He had never been tagged for any of his jobs, nor was there a police file on him anywhere in the world.

Mal had met Parker once, six years before, through a syndicate gun who had earlier worked a job with Parker in Omaha. He recognized Parker and immediately gave him the proposition.

Ordinarily, Parker wouldn't have bothered to listen. But his finances were low, and the job he'd come to Chicago to see about had fallen through. Mal's acquaintanceship with the syndicate gun did serve as a sort of character reference, so he listened. And the idea appealed to him. No law on the trail. That would be a welcome change. And ninety-three grand was a nice pie to split.

Mal introduced Parker and Chester, and Parker thereafter felt even better about the operation. Chester was small-time, but serious and intelligent and close-mouthed. There wasn't any doubt that his information could be trusted nor that he'd be a definite help when the job was pulled.

So far as Parker was concerned, the only thing wrong with the job was Mal. He was a blowhard and a coward, and he could screw things up one way or the other, before, during or after. But Chester was sold on him, and he did have a prior claim to be in the deal, so there was nothing Parker could do about it, except plan to get rid of him as soon as the job was done. Blowhards and cowards were liabilities and Parker had evaded the law this long by systematically canceling his liabilities as soon as possible.

One thing he could do to offset Mal was bring in a couple more men. He convinced Chester that they'd need at least five men to run the operation successfully, and then he contacted Ryan and Sill, good men both, who had also bowed out of the job he'd come to see about and were still in Chicago.

They had three weeks and during that time Parker gradually took over as leader of the string. He arranged for the bankrolling of the job, and set them up with the rental of a small plane. Whether the money was to change hands at Angikuni Lake or the Pacific island, they would need an airplane to get at it. Ryan could fly, and had the necessary licenses. Parker also arranged for the arming of the group.

Less than a week before the exchange was to be made, they boarded the rented plane at Chicago and flew to San Francisco. Once in town, Ryan and Sill shadowed the lawyer, Bleak, until they knew the general pattern of his movements. Then, with one day to go, they hit his apartment at two in the morning.

Bleak was an elderly man, a widower whose financial interests, aside from law practice and munitions trading, included real estate, stock speculation and a piece of an airplane manufacturing concern. He lived alone in his hilltop apartment, except for a Filipino houseboy who slept in and who was killed in his sleep by Ryan.

Bleak didn't want to talk, and Parker put Mal to work on him on the theory that cowards make the best torturers. Mal worked with enthusiasm, and before dawn Bleak had told them all they wanted to know.

The money, he told them, was to be brought north by planes from South America to Canada. Two men from the sellers' group were to be at the island fueling point. The money would be turned over to them there, and they would be guarded by a group of revolutionaries until the planes took off from Canada with the second and last load of munitions. One of the pilots would then radio to the island, and the two men would be allowed to leave with the money.

This part of the operation was tricky, involving radio conversations between individuals on both sides of the transaction, and both sides had worked out code signals to warn of any treachery. Neither group trusted the other very much.

The island, Bleak told them, was a small uninhabited chunk of rock named Keeley's Island, about two hundred miles southwest of San Francisco. During the Second World War, the Coast Guard had maintained a small base there, from which they had operated sub-hunting planes, but for the last fifteen years the place had been deserted. The airfield was still usable, and the necessary gasoline had already been brought out to the island and stored. The two men from Bleak's group were already on the island, and the planes, carrying the money, were due at one o'clock the next morning.

Before they left the apartment, Ryan slit the old man's throat. Otherwise, despite his protestations, he might have gotten on the phone and changed the whole plan.

East of the city, up in the hills, there was a private estate currently unoccupied, the former residence of a movie star. She had owned an airplane, a Piper Cub, and the estate included a small landing strip. The rented plane was there. They drove up there in a stolen Volkswagen Microbus, and Lynn waited in the empty main house while the others boarded the plane and took off for the island.

They found Keeley's Island on the second pass, and landed to gunfire from the rotting control shack. Parker grabbed up one of the machine guns, jumped out of the plane and, while the others kept up a distracting return fire, made a dash for the nearest storage shed. He worked his way around the shed, and raked the control shack until his ammunition was used up. He waited then, and there was only silence. When he pushed his way into the shack, the two defenders were dead.

Ryan maneuvered the plane out of sight, into one of the still-standing hangars, and they sat down to wait. They had arrived at sundown. The dead men had set out small tin cans filled with gasoline along the runway edges, to be lit as markers for the South American planes when they would arrive. Ryan and Sill went out and lit them a little after midnight, and the first plane roared wide-winged into their flickering light at twenty minutes past one. It rolled to a stop on the taxiway off the end of the strip, and the second plane sailed down after it a couple of minutes later.

In the control shack, the five men watched. Mal kept licking his lips and Chester kept studying his rifle to be sure it was really loaded, but the other three waited unmoving.

Three men came out of the first plane, twelve out of the second. Among the twelve were two men carrying bulging briefcases. These two stayed behind the others. The groups met, and came across the field toward the control shack.

"Wait," whispered Parker. "Wait."

The first one was reaching for the doorknob before Parker started firing. He had one machine gun at the window to the left of the door, and Sill had the other at the window to the right. Chester and Mal had rifles at the windows farther away on either side. Ryan was in a barracks, the nearest building to the right, with the third rifle. They each also had a sidearm.

The initial burst of gunfire dropped seven of the fifteen. The rest scattered, the pilots and the men carrying the briefcases scurrying back toward the planes. Parker got one of the briefcase-carriers and Ryan the other. They lay out on the cracked tarmac, the briefcases beside them.

Four of the South Americans ran at the barracks where Ryan was holed in. He got one of them, Sill got two more, and the fourth managed to get into the building, where Ryan hunted him down and finished him.

The battle was brief and one-sided. The last South American took refuge in a storage shed. He had two pistols, and they finally had to burn him out. Then they checked the briefcases to be sure they contained the money, and boarded their own plane. By morning they were back in California, landing on the field behind the estate. There they counted the take, which came to ninety-three thousand, four hundred dollars. After deducting the bankrolling expenses, they were left with just over ninety thousand dollars.

They had already decided on the split. Chester, as the man who had made the job possible, was to get a third: thirty thousand dollars. Mal and Parker each were to get a quarter: twenty-two thousand, five hundred. And Ryan and Sill were to split the last sixth between them: fifteen thousand, seven and a half thousand each. Parker intended to take Mal's slice, too, which would give him a total of forty-five thousand—fifty percent of the take. That was the way it should be.

In the deserted mansion, they made the count and the split, and they were to spend the night there—they were all short on sleep—before heading back to Chicago and separating. Parker planned on getting rid of Mal that night, but he hadn't counted on a double cross, not one involving his wife.

The place was still furnished, and Parker and his wife stayed awake late, in the movie star's bed in the movie star's bedroom. They made love, and smoked cigarettes, and made love. It was always like that after a job. He would be fierce then, and strong, and demanding, and exultant, allowing his emotions the only release he permitted them. Always, for a month or two after a job, they wouldn't skip a night, and often it would be more than once a night. Then gradually his passion would slacken, lessening with their cash reserves until near-celibacy just before the next job. The pattern was always the same, and Lynn had grown used to it, though not without difficulty.

At two in the morning Parker rose from the bed, donned shirt and trousers, and took up the automatic from the stand beside the bed. "I'll go see Mal now," he told her, and headed for the door.

His hand on the knob, she called his name. He turned around, questioning, irritated, and saw the Police Positive in her hand. He had just had time to remember that it had to be either Chester or Mal—the two who'd been given the revolvers—when she pulled the trigger and a heavy punch in his stomach drove the breath and the consciousness out of him.

It was his belt buckle that saved him. Her first shot had hit the buckle, mashing it into his flesh. The gun had jumped in her hand, the next five shots all going over his falling body and into the wood of the door. But she'd fired six shots at him, and she'd seen him fall, and she couldn't believe that he was anything but dead.

He awoke to heat and suffocation. They'd set fire to the house. He was lying on his face and, when he drew his knees up under him in order to stand, pain lanced through his stomach and he saw, in the dim fire-glow, blood on his shirt and trousers.

He thought at first that the bullet was in him, but then he realized what had happened. The buckle, a silver one with a black engraved P, was mashed into a ragged cup-shape. Beneath it, the skin was purplish, and he seemed to be bleeding from his pores. His stomach ached fiercely, as though a heavy iron weight had been crammed into it.

He stood only because he wanted to stand, not because it was possible, and he moved in an agonized side-shuffle, leaning most of his weight against the wall. His chest and shoulders pressed to the wall, he edged slowly out of the room and down the hall.

He should have left the house right away. The far end of the hall was ablaze, and thick smoke filled the stairwell ahead of him. But he had to know which one it was. He made the circuit of the rooms where the others had slept.

Mal was gone. Chester lay dead, his throat cut. Sill was there, dead the same way. Ryan was gone.

Ryan had killed them both—it was his kind of kill. And Mal had given Lynn the revolver, to kill him. Mal had set it up, that was clear, but they'd been in too much of a hurry, wanting to be long gone before daylight. She had fired six shots at him, and he had lain bleeding on the floor, but they hadn't made sure. And that was their mistake.

When he tried to go down the broad staircase into the smoke and the flames, his legs gave out and he fell, rolling and bumping down, landing unconscious again at the foot of the stairs. The heat forced him awake again, and he crawled for the door. There was less smoke at floor level; he could just make out the door, miles away across a flat plain of polished wood. The parallel lines of the flooring rushed away across the plain to converge at the door, like the lined landscapes in a surrealist painting.

He came at last to the door, and crawled up its rococo face to the ornate knob. It took both hands to turn it, and then he flung himself back, falling away, pulling the door open after him. Only then could he crawl over the sill and across the veranda and between two of the pillars and down the two-foot drop to the coolness of the lawn.

After a while, he had strength enough to get on his hands and knees and crawl around the house and down the path toward the landing strip. Midway, in the darkness, he stumbled across a leg, in shoe and trousers. He searched the pockets and found matches. When he lit one, he looked into the dead eyes of Ryan. A chill touched him, a reaction stronger than he was used to when faced with death, and he shook the match out at once. But he had seen the bullet holes in the dead man's chest.

The plane was gone. As he lay on the ground by the landing strip, resting, he heard the faint sound of sirens, and knew he had to get away. This time, he managed to get to his feet and stay on them without holding on to anything. He lurched across the landing strip and into the woods on the other side.

When he came to the fence surrounding the property, he searched until he found a spot where the earth was soft, and scraped away dirt with his hands until he could crawl underneath. Then he went on, staggering downhill and then along a valley until, with false dawn outlining the mountains ahead of him, he fainted.

He spent three days lying in the underbrush, never more than semiconscious. The fact that he lay practically unmoving for three days, and that he didn't take in any food during that time, helped to speed the healing. The next time he came fully awake there was only a dull pain in his stomach, vying unsuccessfully with the fierce ache of hunger. He could stand now with only a faint dizziness, caused by his hunger, and walk with nothing more worrisome than a labored stiffness in his joints. He left the valley, heading westward, trying to find his way back to civilization.

He was a mess. He had no shoes or socks, his shirt and trousers were bloody and filthy and torn, his face and arms were scratched and bruised, and he couldn't walk properly. He came at last to a highway, and walked along it for five minutes before state troopers picked him up. He was too worn down to resist, and they vagged him.

His fifth month on the farm, he wrote a careful letter to a guy he knew in Chicago, asking for information about Mal in a roundabout way. He signed the letter by his prison name,

Ronald Casper, because he knew it would be read by the censor before it was mailed, but in the body of the letter he tried to make it clear who the writer was.

He got an answer three weeks later, an answer as guarded in its phrasing as his question had been, but through the verbiage about nonexistent relatives he got the story. Mal, it seemed, had left Chicago some time ago, with a woman who could only have been Lynn. He had apparently squared himself with the syndicate and had been taken back into the fold. He had been recently seen in New York, spending heavily and living the good life. Lynn was still with him.

So Parker waited, and when his chance came he took it. He killed a guard rather than wait the two more months until they would have released him anyway. He had to get moving. He wanted Mal Resnick—he wanted him between his hands. Not the money back. Not Lynn back. Just Mal, between his hands.

He headed first for Palm Springs, but the fifteen hundred dollars he'd had in the hotel safe there was gone. Lynn had taken it. He knew without checking that she'd cleaned out his other reserves, too.

He wasn't a petty thief or a hobo. He didn't have the background or the training or the temperament for it. He fared badly coming across the country, but he stayed alive. He jackrolled for eating money, traveled by truck when he could get a lift and by train when he couldn't, and headed east. He avoided the people he knew, and regretted having written the friend in Chicago.

He didn't want Mal to know he was alive. He didn't want Mal spooked and on the run. He wanted him easy and content, a fat cat. He wanted him just sitting there, grinning, waiting for Parker's hands.

Two

1

Mal was sitting there, grinning, waiting for Parker's hands. He didn't know he was waiting for Parker: he thought he was waiting for a chick named Pearl, a junkie with only two bad habits. It was the other habit that interested Mal right now. He sat there in his dressing gown from Japan with a silk dragon brocaded on the back, and he grinned, and he waited for Pearl and Parker.

There was the living room of his suite in the Outfit hotel. The Outfit hotel was a respectable-looking stone structure on Park Avenue in the Fifties, with the name *Oakwood Arms* on the marquee. The building was eleven stories high, with two L-wings jutting back toward Lexington Avenue, and eight of its eleven stories held innocent, respectable, well-paying guests. The guests on floors one and two and three were not innocent, not respectable, and not well paying. They were Outfit men, and they called the Oakwood Arms home. On the third floor were the permanents, Mal Resnick and the other New York workers who had chosen to live here where questions were never asked because the answers were already known. The second floor was partly filled with other permanents and partly reserved for transients, visiting Outfit men from other parts of the country or occasionally from overseas, in town for conference or vacation. When a junketing syndicate man told his lieutenants, "I'll be staying with the Outfit while I'm in New York," they knew he meant the Oakwood Arms.

On the first floor were the conference rooms and bars and ballrooms and dens which the innocent, respectable, well-paying guests never saw. No illegality was ever committed in the Outfit hotel, no wanted man was ever seen to enter or leave the place. No police spy was ever hired by the management, whose security check of its prospective employees would have been the envy of the government boys at Los Alamos.

The police had never raided the place, probably realizing it would be a waste of time, but the hotel was ready for even that emergency. Well-concealed side exits on the first three floors led into adjoining buildings, and the three desk clerks were prepared to alert the Outfit guests before the law could even get into the elevators.

The hotel had only gradually developed to the plush respectability and safety it now enjoyed. Early during Prohibition it had been bought by the liquor syndicate as a plant, where booze could be stored with relative safety at a location pleasantly close to the speakeasies of midtown. During those early years no one made much of an effort to front the place as a normal hotel, but after the racket-busters began to crack down, and the place was raided a few times, the syndicate realized the building could only be useful if it did a good job of pretending to be what it was not. The remaining liquor was pulled out, the hotel was paper-sold to a legit front man, and new employees were brought in who didn't know a thing about the place's actual owners or purposes, and for six years the hotel was a sleeper, bringing the syndicate nothing but a small legitimate profit.

In 1930, with the respectable front firmly established, the Oakwood Arms became once more a plant, but this time the mob used it more carefully and more quietly. With the end of Prohibition in 1933, the hotel embarked on its new career as a location for business conferences, as the liquor syndicates merged and disbanded and remerged again in a frantic reshuffling of influence and interest, converting from suddenly legal liquor to still profitably illegal items like gambling, unionizing, prostitution and narcotics.

In the years since, the Oakwood Arms had slowly developed its role in Outfit affairs. It was used more as a permanent or temporary residence for Outfit executives than for any other reason, with occasional conferences and parties as well. Since the Apalachin fiasco of 1957, more and more out-of-town elements of the Outfit had been using the hotel as a safe meeting place. It was quiet, it was well run, and it was guaranteed free from trouble with the law.

So it was with perfect nonchalance that Mal Resnick sat in the living room of his third-floor suite in the hotel, in his dressing gown from Japan, and waited for Pearl, the girl with only two bad habits.

Mal was a beefy man, short and heavy-set, with broad, soft, sloping shoulders and a wide paunch, short thick legs and arms, and a heavy head set square on a thick neck. In the old days, his hands had been large and rough, work coarsened, but now they were only pudgy, the flesh packed thick around the finger bones, the skin soft and pink. He was a cab driver, with a cab driver's body and a cab driver's movements, and nothing would ever change that.

Around him were the symbols of his success, the stereo hi-fi built into the wall, the well-stocked bar, the deep-piled carpet and plush armchairs and sofas. His was a two-room suite, living room and bedroom only, proclaiming him still on one of the lower rungs as an Outfit executive. But the fact that he could live here at all proclaimed even louder that he had power within the mob, that he had made it: he wasn't a goon or a hanger-on, he was one of the Boys.

He looked at his watch and saw that it was quarter after seven. That meant that Pearl was fifteen minutes late, and Mal grinned again. Pearl was late, Pearl would be punished. She knew that, and she would come anyway—and whatever he decided the punishment should be, she would go along with it.

It occurred to him sometimes that she was probably so insensitized by drugs that his punishments meant practically nothing to her, but he rejected the idea. She felt it, by God. When Mal put his hands on her to make her hurt, she hurt. And if it took more to break through the deadening of the heroin in Pearl's system, so much the better. Mal had the patience, Mal had the time, and Mal had the incentive.

He looked at his watch again, saw that it was twenty minutes past seven, and the phone rang. His right hand reached out negligently, expecting it was Pearl calling in resigned panic from some phone booth somewhere in the world, and he brought the phone lazily to his ear. "Mal," he said.

"Mal, this is Fred Haskell. I'm sorry to call you at home, but—"

"Don't be sorry, sweetie. Just don't call."

"But," said Haskell, "I thought maybe this was important. Maybe I ought to call you right away."

Haskell was a junior executive, a rung or two beneath Mal in the Outfit chain of command. Mal still remembered too clearly the last time he'd loused himself up by a stupid mistake on Outfit business, so he didn't throw his weight around now. He said instead, "Something about business, Fred?"

"I'm not sure. I got a call from that cab guy out in Brooklyn. Stegman. He wanted to get in touch with you."

Mal frowned. He didn't like to be reminded of Stegman or of Lynn or of anything else connected with that operation. "You didn't give him my number, sweetie," he said.

"Hell no, Mal—you know me. I told him I hadn't seen you in months."

"Good boy."

"So he said I should ask around. He said he had to get in touch with you, it was important."

Mal's frown deepened. Was that stuff coming back to plague him? It couldn't. Unless maybe Lynn was suddenly deciding she wanted more dough.

He ought to drop that bitch, she wasn't worth it. A grand a month was heavy money; he couldn't really afford it. And what did he get from her? Nothing. He put it to her a few times, and every damn time she just lay there like a board and closed her eyes and went a million miles away somewhere. He tried to hurt her, and she hurt easy, but he couldn't reach her any other way at all, and the hell with that.

Was she a danger to him? If he was to drop her now, what the hell could she do? Not a damn thing. She didn't know where he was, and even if she did he had nothing to fear from her physically. And if she spread the word about where and how he'd gotten the dough to pay back the Outfit, all he had to do was say she was a lying, vindictive bitch, he'd kept her for a while and then gotten tired of her and she was trying to get even. Nobody would listen to her.

So why keep her around? If it was conscience money, it was stupid. And it couldn't be anything else.

So he made his decision. If she wants more dough, I drop her. To Haskell he said, "Did he tell you what it was?"

"He said some guy had come around looking for you. Killed some broad and then came around wanting you."

"Some *guy*?" Ryan? No, he was dead. They were all dead. One of the South Americans? How the hell could they have found out who was in on the hijack? Somebody from the Outfit selling the guns? There was no way for them to connect him with the deal either. "What did this guy look like?"

"He didn't tell me. He just said some guy came around talking mean and wanting you."

"Talking mean. The hell with that."

"I thought you ought to know about it, Mal, you know what I mean?"

"Yeah, yeah, you done right. Listen, I want to talk to that son of a bitch."

"Stegman?"

"Who else? Set up a meeting."

"At your place?"

"Go to hell, sweetie. I'll meet him at Landau's, by the bridge. In back."

"Landau's, by the bridge."

"At nine o'clock."

"Tonight?"

"When the hell else, idiot?"

"I'm not sure I can get in touch with him, Mal, that's the only thing."

"Get in touch with him, sweetie. Do it. That lousy cab company of his is working now."

"Okay, Mal, I'll try."

"Don't try, sweetie. Do."

Mal slammed the phone onto the hook and surged out of the chair. Who was it? Who the hell was it?

He strode across the living room, throwing off his dressing gown as he went. Beneath it, his chunky body was nude, heavy and fat-rolled, with an even sunlamp tan.

He threw on his clothing, muttering to himself, remembering names and faces, trying to figure out who it had been. Killed a broad and came looking for Mal. Killed a broad and came looking—

Killed Lynn.

His suit and shoes on, he came out to the living room again, staggering slightly, as the realization hit him. Killed Lynn. It had to be, it was the only broad connecting him to Stegman. Killed Lynn.

Oh, sweet Jesus Christ in Heaven!

The doorbell rang.

He stood frozen, staring at the door. The bell rang again and he bellowed, "Who is it? What do you want?"

Her answer came faint through the door. "It's me, honey. It's Pearl."

He pulled open the door and she came in, her mouth open, ready with excuses.

"It's Parker," he said, and hit her twice in the stomach. She fell retching to the floor, and he stepped on her back on the way out.

2

By day, the shadow of the Manhattan Bridge lies on the windows of Landau's Bar and Grill. By night, there are too many shadows to pick out the source of any one.

Mal parked his Outfit car two blocks away and walked through the Dutch slum to Landau's. The regulars hunched at the bar watched him in the back mirror as he walked down the length of the place, and they disliked him because he wore a suit and tie. But they knew better than to turn around, to speak or gesture or notice him in any way. They knew, vaguely, that Landau's was different from the other bars in the neighborhood, that it led some sort of double life. Suits and ties congregated in the back room every once in a while, and it was best to leave them alone.

Stegman was already there, and nervous. He got up from the small room's one table when Mal came in, and said, "Jesus, am I glad to see you! This place is a hole."

Mal shut the door. "What did he look like?"

"What? Big. A mean-looking bastard, Mal. He braced me

without a gun or a knife or anything. He said if he had to he'd kill me with his hands, and I swear to Christ I believed him."

"It's Parker," said Mal to himself.

"He had big hands, Mal." Stegman held up his own hands, claw-curved. "The veins stuck out all over them."

"The son of a bitch," said Mal.

"I tell you, I wouldn't want him after *me*."

"Shut up!" Mal glared, his hands closing into fists. "What am I, a nobody? I got friends."

"Sure you have, Mal."

"Am I supposed to be afraid of the son of a bitch? He couldn't get near me."

Stegman licked his lips. "I thought you'd want to know about it, Mal."

"All I have to do is point," said Mal. "I pick up the phone and I say his name, and he's a dead man. And this time he stays dead."

"Sure. I thought you'd want to know so you could take care of it."

Mal crossed suddenly to the table, scraping the chair out and plumping down into it. "Sit down," he said. "Tell me what he said. What did he say about me?"

Stegman sat across the table, his hands palm down on the table top. They trembled slightly anyway. "He said you could stop paying off the girl, she was dead. She was in the morgue. He said he was looking for you. That's all."

"Not who he was? Not why?"

"Nothing. Just what I said."

"And he told you if you saw me you should let him know."

Stegman shook his head. "No, he didn't. He just let it go."

The bartender pushed open the door, stuck his head in. "You gents want anything?"

"A beer," said Stegman.

"Nothing," said Mal. "Peace and quiet."

The bartender waited, looking at Stegman. "Beer or no beer?"

Stegman shrugged, awkwardly. "No beer," he said. "Later maybe."

"We'll let you know," said Mal.

The bartender went away, and Stegman said, "That's all there was, Mal. I told you everything."

"What did you tell him?"

"Nothing. What could I tell him? I didn't know where you were, what could I tell him?"

"What about the money?"

Stegman nodded quickly. "Yeah, I told him about that. About the checking account. He wanted to know about that, how I got the money."

Mal gnawed on his lower lip, looking across the room. "Could he trace me through that? The statements go to you. The bank wouldn't tell him nothing."

"That's what I figured," said Stegman eagerly. "It wouldn't hurt to tell him the truth. What could he do?"

"I don't know. He used to be dead, and now he isn't. I don't know what he could do. What else did you tell him?"

"Nothing, Mal." Stegman spread his hands. "What could I tell him? I didn't know anything else."

"Then why didn't he kill you?"

Stegman blinked. "He must of believed me."

"You gave him something else. To save your own stinking skin, you gave him something else. A name, maybe—somebody who knows where to find me."

"I swear to Christ, Mal—"

"Haskell's name, maybe. Didn't you?"

"On my mother, Mal—"

"Up your mother. Did you or didn't you?" Mal waved a hand, keeping Stegman from answering. "Wait a minute. Don't cover yourself for nothing. I'm not down on you, I know the way that bastard comes on. If you told him about Haskell, I want Haskell to be ready for him, that's all—you got nothing to worry about."

"I didn't tell him about Haskell," said Stegman. "I didn't give him any names at all, I swear it."

"What, then? You told him I was for sure in New York."

The denial hung on Stegman's lips, then fell back into his throat. He nodded. "I had to give him something, Mal," he said. "He kept flexing those goddam hands of his."

"All right. All right." Mal nodded, his whole torso moving. "That was good, Art, don't worry about it. That means he'll stick around town. That wasn't bad."

"I just had to give him something, that's all, so he wouldn't think I was holding out on him."

"That's all right. Just so you don't hold out on me either. Where did he say to contact him?"

"He didn't, Mal. Jesus, I'm not lying. I wasn't even going to give you the word at all, only we been friends—"

"Bushwah. You were afraid he'd get to me, and I'd find out."

"Mal, we been friends."

"Where are you supposed to call? If you run into me, you're supposed to call him."

Stegman's head shook back and forth. "He didn't even suggest it, Mal. He didn't even suggest it."

Mal pondered, chewing his lower lip, thinking it over. Finally he said, "Okay. That's the way he'd work. He wouldn't trust you either."

"You can trust me, Mal. For Christ's sake—"

"Yeah, I know—we're friends."

"We been friends for years, Mal."

"You had him. And you let him go." Mal nodded. "All right, Art. Now find him again."

Stegman raised his hands. "What? How do I do that? I don't know nothing about him."

"I don't care how you do it, just do it."

"I wouldn't know how to start, Mal. For Christ's sake, give me a break."

"I'm giving you a break, you bastard. I'm giving you a chance to make up for doing it wrong the first time."

"Mal, there just isn't any way—"

Mal leaned forward over the table. "Sweetie," he said, "there's got to be a way. You hear me? I got friends, and that means there's got to be a way. Unless maybe you want to drive all your cabs yourself."

Stegman opened his mouth to argue some more, but then he closed it again and looked down at the table. "I'll try, Mal," he said. "I don't know how the hell I'll do it, but I'll try."

"Good boy." Mal leaned back, smiling. "There's one of him. I got the whole Outfit on my side. What can he do?"

"Sure, Mal."

"Get us a couple beers, Artie."

Stegman got hurriedly to his feet. "Right away, Mal. Never mind, I'll spring."

Mal hadn't reached for his wallet at all.

3

Mal walked down the third-floor hall of the Outfit hotel, and knocked at the door of suite 312. He waited, and when the blond girl in the red bra and the pink toreador pants opened the door, he said, "I want to talk to Phil. Tell him Mal Resnick."

"Okay." She closed the door again, leaving him in the hall. He lit a cigarette and then, remembering Phil's asthma, he looked around for a place to put it out again. The floor was deep-pile carpeted, and the nearest sand urn was way down by the elevators. Mal hurried down and stubbed out the cigarette. He was halfway back when the door opened again, and the blonde stepped out to look for him. He waved and trotted, feeling like a fool.

She watched him deadpan, and turned away when he got to the door. He followed her inside, panting slightly, and over her shoulder she said, "Close the door."

"Sure."

"Phil says to sit down out here. He'll be along in a minute."

"Okay. Thanks."

She went away, deeper into the suite, not looking back at him, and Mal settled in the white sofa, grateful for the chance to catch his breath.

He looked around at the living room, which was nearly twice as big as his own and even more opulently furnished. Phil had four rooms, and they were all like this. Phil was way up in the chain of command, the highest man Mal could go to directly. Some day, he told himself, he'd have four rooms like this, and a blonde like that piece in the red bra. That was good stuff.

He wouldn't have any more bags like that Pearl. Nothing but good stuff, filling red bras, with tight butts in pink toreador pants, and flat bellies with that little bump at the lower part of the abdomen. That was the kind of thing he wanted, and that was the kind of thing he was due for. He was watching his step, he was doing his job, and he was proving his mettle. They had him slated for big things, and he knew it.

Phil kept him waiting ten minutes. When he finally came out, he wore nothing but a pair of gray slacks. A lipstick smudge was clearly outlined against the skin of his chest, just under the left nipple. Mal looked at him, and knew that Phil kept him waiting while he tore off a piece. With that blonde. Mal kept his face blank. He could wait.

The day was coming when they'd wait for him in his living room while he tore off a piece with something like that. He had it already, underlings, guys who waited when he said to wait, and he had broads. But he was going to have better.

What could Parker do against him? He was set, he was on the escalator, he was riding up. What could that one-man son of a bitch do?

Phil said, "How ya doing, Mal?" and turned his back to go

over to the bar and make himself a drink. Coming back, he said, "You want something? The fixings are there."

"Thanks, Phil."

Mal made himself a quick drink, good Scotch and an ice cube and a splash of Vichy. He came back and Phil was stretched out on the sofa, so he took the leather chair instead.

Phil sipped at his drink. "You look nervous, Mal. Something wrong with the operation?"

"No, no, nothing like that. Smooth as silk, Phil. I keep everything smooth as silk, you know that."

"Sure. You're a good manager type, Mal."

Mal grinned. "Thanks. What I wanted, I was wondering if you could set me up an appointment with Mr. Fairfax."

"Justin?" Phil raised an eyebrow, then shook his head. "Sorry, buddy," he said. "Justin is down in Florida right now."

"Mr. Carter, then."

"Mr. Carter," repeated Phil. "Nothing but the best, huh, Mal? Sure it isn't something I could handle?"

This was tricky. Phil could help him; Phil could hurt him— in the job, in the career. Mal grinned awkwardly, saying, "This isn't really Outfit business, Phil. Not directly. It's something personal. But I'd need to talk to Mr. Fairfax or Mr. Carter."

Phil considered, swirling the ice cubes in his glass. Then he said, "I'll see what I can do for you, Mal. I don't promise anything, you understand that, but I'll see what I can do."

"I'd appreciate it, Phil, I really would."

"Now," said Phil, "I'll have to know what it's all about. You know that. I can't go to Fred Carter and say, 'This fella Mal Resnick—he's one of the boys—he wants to see you,' and not know what it's all about. You know that. He'll say, 'Phil, what does this boy want?' You see what I mean?"

Mal chewed on his lower lip. "It's this way," he said. "There's this guy, he's got it in for me."

"An Outfit boy?"

"No, no—outside the Outfit."

Phil nodded. "Okay."

"Anyway, I thought he was dead. But all of a sudden, he's around, he's looking for me."

"And what is it you want, Mal? You can't handle this guy yourself?"

"Sure I can. But I don't know where he is. He's somewhere in town, and I don't know where. Now, he's poking his nose in, he's asking questions, he's stirring things up. I want to find this guy, you see what I mean? Before he rocks the boat."

"You want us to help you find him, is that it? And then you'll take care of him yourself."

"Sure. That's it. I fight my own battles, Phil. But I need help finding the bastard."

"What is this guy? You say he ain't Outfit."

"He's a heister, a hijacker. An independent."

"He's got a string with him?"

Mal didn't know for sure, one way or the other. Figuring Parker, probably not. He'd want to take care of this by himself. "No string. He's a loner."

Phil finished his drink, taking his time, and then got to his feet. "All right, buddy," he said. "I'll talk to Mr. Carter. You stick close to your room. Okay?"

Mal stood, gulping the rest of his Scotch and Vichy. "Will do," he said. "Thanks a lot, Phil."

"Any time, buddy." Phil smiled and patted his shoulder. "Any time you've got a problem, pal, you come talk it over with me. Right?"

"Sure, Phil. Thanks."

"Right. And now if you'll excuse me, buddy, I've got a little something—"

"Oh, sure," said Mal. "Sure thing." He started for the door, realized the empty glass was still in his hand, and detoured to the bar. Then he smiled quickly at Phil, who stood there in the middle of the room waiting for him to go, and left.

4

*T*he office building was thirty-seven stories high. In gold letters on the frosted glass door of 706 were the words: FREDERICK CARTER, Investments. Mal pushed open the door and entered an empty anteroom. A bell rang faintly as he closed the door.

Two sofas, two standing lamps, two end tables, a stack of back issues of *U.S. News & World Report.* An unmarked wooden door across the room. Mal stood hesitating, wondering whether or not to sit down and wait, when the door opened and a tall broad-shouldered man, who looked like a movie cowboy, but wore a dark gray business suit, came out and closed the door again after him. Mal heard the lock click shut.

The man said, "Can I help you?" There was a trace of roughness left in a voice that tried to be soft.

Mal said, "I'm Mal Resnick. I have an appointment with Mr. Carter."

"Resnick," said the man. "Yes, I remember. Turn around, please."

Mal turned around, and the man came over to pat him briefly, frisking him. His wallet was slipped out of his pocket, his driver's license read, and the wallet put back. "All right," said the man. "Come with me."

Mal turned around again, glad he'd resisted the impulse to wear a gun—with Parker somewhere in New York, maybe he'd need one, maybe they'd just bump into each other on the street or something—and waited while the man unlocked the door and led the way through.

They crossed a gray office with functional gray furnishings, and through another door to a kind of living room–bar.

"Wait here. Please do not drink," the man said, unsmiling.

Mal waited, and after a couple of minutes the man came back, holding the inner door open and saying, "Mr. Carter will see you now."

"Thank you."

Mal went into Mr. Carter's office. The man closed the door again and went over to sit impassive in a corner to the right. Mr. Carter said, "Come on in, Resnick. Sit down."

Mr. Carter was an impressive man. His resemblance to Louis Calhern was startling. Sitting behind a massive mahogany desk, he brought to mind visions of Wall Street and high finance, rails and steel and banking. Law books and economic treatises filled the glass-doored bookshelves. Photographs, unsigned, of presidents were spotted around the walls.

He motioned now to a brown leather chair in front of his desk, and Mal settled into it promptly, trying to sit tall and alert. "Phil tells me you have a personal problem you want us to help you with. Is that right?"

Mal swallowed. It wasn't a good beginning. "Well, it's a personal problem, but I thought it might hurt the Outfit if this guy was to keep nosing around."

Mr. Carter made a tent of his fingers. "That's a possibility," he said. "Now there are three possible ways to handle this situation." He ticked them off on his fingers. "First, we could give you the assistance you ask for. Second, we could ignore the problem and let you handle it yourself, as best you may. Third, if it seemed that there actually was a danger to the smooth operation of our organization, we could have you replaced."

Mal blinked, and looked instinctively over his shoulder at the other man, but he was still just sitting there, impassive.

"Each of these alternatives," Mr. Carter went on quietly, "has its advantages. We have an investment in you, Resnick, of time and money and training. After one mistake in Chicago, you've done very well in the organization. If we choose our first alternative, and give you our assistance, we'll be protecting our investment in you, which is always good business policy."

"I'd appreciate it, Mr. Carter," Mal said hurriedly. "I'd do good work, you'd never regret it."

"If we choose our second alternative," Mr. Carter said, ignoring him, "that of ignoring the problem and leaving it to your own devices, there is another advantage to consider. A man in our organization, Resnick, has to be tough and self-reliant. Were you to handle this problem completely on your own, you would leave no doubt in anyone's mind that you were the kind of man we want, the kind of man who could go places in our organization."

Mal nodded briskly. "I want to handle it myself, Mr. Carter," he said. "All I want is some help finding this guy. Once he's spotted, I can take care of it myself."

"However," said Mr. Carter, "there is always that business in Chicago. You made good on that, you paid us back for your blunder. But still the blunder did happen. And it leaves a question in our minds. Perhaps you don't have the mettle we require. You're a good administrator in your area, but being a good administrator is not enough. Perhaps the blunder in Chicago—and the fact that you have allowed an area of your personal life to become a possible danger to the organization—are indications that you are not our kind of man. In that case, our most profitable move would be to have you eliminated as a factor in the organization. That would automatically remove the external danger you have brought to us."

Mal sat silent, every nerve tense. His lips trembled, but no arguments came to his mind.

Mr. Carter studied the tent of his fingers. His lips pursed and relaxed, pursed and relaxed. Finally, he raised his eyes and said, "Before making my decision, perhaps I'd better know more about your problem. According to Phil, there is a man unconnected with the organization who has a grudge against you, and who has come to New York looking for you, apparently to kill you. You also say that he is alone, and that he is a professional robber. Is that right?"

Mal nodded. "That's right. He does payroll jobs, banks, things like that."

"What is his name?"

"Parker."

Mr. Carter frowned. "Doesn't he have a first name?"

"I don't know it, Mr. Carter. He never called himself anything but Parker. His wife must of known it, but she never told me. I never thought to ask."

"And does this wife of Parker's have something to do with the grudge?"

"Yes, sir."

"In other words, you are being hunted by a cuckolded husband, is that it?"

Mal considered, thinking fast. If he said yes, there wouldn't be any embarrassing questions about that hijacking job. But would the Outfit think it important enough to help a guy having trouble with some broad's husband? Probably not. Mal took a deep breath. "There's more to it than that, Mr. Carter," he said.

"Yes. I thought there must be. Where did you get the eighty thousand dollars, Resnick?"

"Mr. Carter, I—"

"That's what this man is here for, isn't it? The eighty thousand dollars you paid us back?"

Mal gnawed his lip. "Yes."

Mr. Carter sat back, his leather chair creaking expensively. "We never asked you where you got that money, Resnick," he said. "It wasn't our business. You owed us a debt, and you paid it, and we gave you a second chance. Now it appears that it is our business after all. Where did you get the money, Resnick?"

"A—a heist. A holdup, Mr. Carter."

"And who was held up? This man Parker?"

"No, sir."

"He was part of the gang that performed the holdup?"

"Yes, sir."

Mr. Carter nodded, gazing over Mal's head at the opposite wall. "You betrayed your associate for profit," he said. "Not always a reprehensible action, if there was a sensible motive. And this time there was a sensible motive. You wanted to repay us for your blunder."

"That's right, Mr. Carter." Mal leaned forward eagerly in his chair. "I set the thing up, you see, and this guy Parker tried a double cross first. But it didn't work, and I switched it back on him."

"You shouldn't have left him alive, Resnick," Mr. Carter said. "That was a serious error of judgment."

"I thought he was dead, Mr. Carter. I shot him, and he sure as hell *looked* dead. And then I set fire to the house he was in."

"I see." Mr. Carter spread his hands palm down on the green blotter atop his desk and considered his fingernails. "There is one more matter," he said. "Just where did this holdup take place?"

Mal had already seen that question coming, and he knew that this time the truth would be more dangerous than any lie. There was always the chance—and a pretty good chance at that—that either Mr. Carter himself or some friend of his had invested in that munitions deal. It was time for a lie.

But Mr. Carter just might check the lie. Mal remembered Parker mentioning that he and Ryan had worked together on a job in Des Moines not long before the island job. Mal didn't know the details but it had taken place and it was the only other one he knew. So he said, "In Des Moines, Mr. Carter, about a year and a half ago. A payroll job."

"I see. And you left with Parker's share of the money and also with Parker's wife, is that it?"

Mal nodded. "Yes, sir."

Mr. Carter permitted himself a wintry smile. "His grudge, therefore," he said, "is perfectly understandable."

"It was him or me, Mr. Carter."

"Of course. Is Mrs. Parker still with you?"

"No, sir. We broke up about three months ago. I heard he killed her yesterday."

"Killed her? Do you suppose he found out first where to find you?"

"She didn't know, Mr. Carter."

"You're sure of that?"

"Yes, sir."

"All right." Mr. Carter made a tent of his fingers again, and studied the fingertips. His lips pursed and relaxed, fishlike, and the silence in the room lengthened. The silent man in the corner shifted position, causing a slight rustle, and Mal jumped, his head snapping around, his eyes staring. He breathed again when he saw that the man was still just sitting there, impassive, smoking a cigarette.

Mal wanted a cigarette. He wanted one badly. But he didn't think it would be right to light one. He licked his lips and waited.

Finally, Mr. Carter looked up. "If you remember," he said, "we have three possible choices." He ticked them off on his fingers. "Assist you, leave you to your own devices, or eliminate you from the organization. For the moment, I think we will pursue number two. If you manage to handle this problem yourself, so much the better. If you find you're having too much difficulty, come back and we'll talk it over, and decide whether we should shift to choice one or choice three." His wintry smile came out again. "I think that's our best decision for now."

Mal got unsteadily to his feet, a growing chill in the pit of his stomach. "Thank you, Mr. Carter."

"That's perfectly all right. Any time. Oh, and Resnick. You are responsible for the work of a group within the organization. That group has a sufficient workload. They won't be available to help you in this personal matter."

"No, sir," said Mal.

"One other thing. Perhaps it would be best, until this matter is settled one way or the other, if you were to move out of the Oakwood Arms. Your suite will be saved for you, of course. We wouldn't want any unpleasantness at the hotel. You understand?"

"Yes, sir," said Mal.

The silent man accompanied him to the outer door.

5

Mal stood at the phone, counting the rings. On the tenth, he jammed his thumb on the cradle button, breaking the connection, and dialed another number. Pearl wasn't at home. Maybe she was at that crummy bar again.

She wasn't. The bartender recognized his voice and told him no, Pearl wasn't there. It irritated him that the bartender recognized his voice. He'd been relying on Pearl too much, he should get hold of something else.

It occurred to him that she might be at the hotel, waiting for him, not knowing that he'd moved, or that at least he could leave a message for her there at the desk. But the hell with it. He wanted something else, something good. Like that blonde of Phil's.

He hesitated, almost calling the Oakwood Arms anyway, but finally dialing a different number. A woman answered, a woman with a husky cigarette-raw voice, and he said, "Mal Resnick, Irma. I could use a girl."

"Couldn't we all, honey? What's your price range?"

"I want something good, Irma," he said, visualizing what he wanted. "A blonde, something really good. For all night."

"Mal, honey," she said, "it's been a while since you called. There's been something I've wanted to say to you."

"What?"

"The envelope, honey. The last two girls complained to me. There wasn't enough in the envelope."

He laughed, feeling not at all like laughing. "What the hell, Irma, discount to a fellow worker in the Outfit, right?"

"Wrong, honey. The girls got to make a living too. They got their price, they want to stick with customers who pay the price, you see what I mean?"

Mal was in no mood to argue. "All right," he said abruptly. "All right, all right. I'll pay a hundred cents on the dollar. Satisfied?"

"Rarely, honey. Now I asked you, what price range?"

"I told you what I wanted. A blonde, something really good. Young, Irma, young and stacked."

"You are talking about a hundred dollars, honey."

Mal frowned and gnawed his lip, then nodded convulsively. "All right," he said. "A hundred. For the night."

"What else? You're at the Outfit, aren't you?"

"No, I moved. The St. David on 57th Street. Room 516."

"You want to take her out to dinner, a show, anything like that?"

"I want her *here,* Irma. In the rack, you follow me?"

Irma laughed throatily. "An athletic blonde," she said. "She'll be there by eight o'clock."

"Fine."

Mal hung up, and turned around to face the room, but there wasn't any bar in it. Thirty-two dollars a day, and no bar. He turned back and called room service. Two bottles, glasses, ice. They'd be right up.

It was barely seven o'clock. He had an hour to kill. He paced the room, disgusted. A hundred dollars for a lay: that was disgusting. Parker coming back from the dead: that was disgusting. Getting screwed up this way with the Outfit: that was disgusting. Even the room was disgusting.

The room was one of four. He wasn't sure what had made him do that, splurge on a four-room suite costing thirty-two dollars a day, any more than he was sure why he was throwing away a hundred dollars on a broad who couldn't possibly do any more for him than Pearl would. And who would, probably, since they would be strangers, do even less.

But he had splurged, reason or no reason he had splurged, on the girl and on the suite. Knowing that neither could be worth it.

The suite, for instance. This living room. It was old. The paint was new, the furnishings and fixtures were new, the prints on the walls were new, but beneath it all the room was old, and in the way of hotel rooms the oldness managed to gleam dirtily through the new overlay. And besides being old, it was impersonal. The suite at the Outfit hotel was *his,* it was where he lived. This suite wasn't lived in by anybody, now or ever, any more than a compartment in a Pullman car was lived in. It could be occupied, but it couldn't be lived in.

The girl would be the same way.

He was doing things wrong, he was making stupid mistakes, and what made it worse was the fact that he knew it. The knowledge that Parker was alive had rattled him more than he liked to admit. Going to Mr. Carter, for instance. He'd gained nothing, and maybe he'd lost.

Now Mr. Carter was watching him. Now he had to get Parker, not just avoid him but *get* him. This was a test and the Outfit was watching, and if he failed now he was through forever. This time he was too far up the chain of command to just be put out in the street. This time they would have to kill him.

He had to work alone. If he hadn't gone to Mr. Carter, he could have used some of the boys in his group, even given one of them the assignment of finishing Parker. Now he'd screwed up that chance, too. He had to work alone.

Stegman wouldn't find Parker, he knew that. Stegman couldn't possibly find Parker. It was up to him, completely up to him.

Suddenly he stopped his pacing, struck with an idea. There *was* a way to use the Outfit. It was dangerous as hell, but he could do it. He'd have to do it. There wasn't any other way.

He hurried across the room to the telephone and quickly dialed a number. When Fred Haskell answered, he said, "Fred, I want you to pass a word around for me."

"Sure, Mal. Anything you say. How'd it go with Stegman?"

"Fine, fine. It's about that. This guy who's looking for me, his name is Parker. Now I've moved out of the Outfit for a while, I'm staying at the St. David on 57th, room 516. You spread the word around. If anybody asks for me, asks any of the guys, this Parker shows up, tell him where I am. You got that?"

"You want us to tell him?"

"Right. Not easy, not right off the bat, or he'll smell something fishy. But let him know where I am. Then call me right away. You got that? They don't call you, they call me."

"Okay, Mal. Whatever you say."

"Make sure they call me right away."

"I'll tell them, Mal."

"Okay."

Mal hung up and took a deep breath. All right. When the time came, he knew a couple of guys he could hire to hang around with him. They worked for the Outfit sometimes, sometimes not—they were like free-lancers. It wouldn't be the same as using Outfit people.

There was a knock at the door. Mal started, eyes jerking involuntarily to the phone. He called, "Who is it?"

"Room service."

"Hold it. Hold on a second."

The gun was in the bedroom, on the bed, next to the suitcase. He hurried in, picked it up, brought it back to the living room with him. The pocket of the dressing gown was large; the gun was a smallish .32, an English make. He held tightly to the gun in his pocket and opened the door.

A kid in a red and black bellboy uniform wheeled in a chrome cart with the liquor and mix and glasses and ice. Mal closed the door after him, and only then relaxed his grip on the gun. He fumbled in the bottom of his pocket, past the gun, and his fingers found two quarters. They went into the bellboy's open hand, and Mal clutched the gun again as he opened the door for the bellboy to go out. There was no one else in the hall.

Alone again, he made himself a drink, glancing at the phone. He looked at his watch and it was only quarter after seven. Forty-five minutes. Forty-five minutes. If she was early, she'd get an extra ten.

He went into the bedroom and cleared the suitcase off the bed and pulled the spread down. He kept standing looking at the bed. His right hand clutched the gun in his pocket.

6

She was only five minutes early, so he decided the hell with the extra ten. When she knocked at the door, he went through the same routine as with the bellboy, holding hard to the gun in his pocket, calling through the door. He didn't hear what she answered, but it was a female voice so he opened the door, and she smiled at him and came in.

She was a knockout. Better than Phil's, a million times better. She looked like Vassar maybe, or some hotshot's private secretary on Madison Avenue, or a starlet on the Grace Kelly line.

She was a blonde, like he'd asked for, with medium-short pale hair in one of those television hairdos. Perched atop the hairdo was a black box hat with a little veil. She wore a gray suit and a green silk scarf, like a photo in *Vogue.*

Her legs were long and slender, sheathed in sheer nylon, shod in green high heels. She walked like a model, one foot directly in front of the other, the pelvis rotating back and forth, her left arm and green-gloved hand swinging straight at her side in short arcs, her right hand, bare, holding her tiny black purse and other green glove to her body, just below her breast.

Her face had been chiseled with care, honed and smoothed to creamy perfection, slender brows arched over green eyes, aquiline nose, soft-lipped mouth with just a trace of lipstick, long slender throat and cameo shoulders.

He looked at her and he knew he would never have better. If he lived a hundred years, he'd never have anything again as good as this. Better in the rack, maybe, he didn't know about that, but not better looking, not more desirable or more perfect than this.

She smiled, stepping across the threshold with her model's walk, saying, "Hello, Mal. I'm Linda," extending her gloved left hand to him, palm down, fingers curved slightly. Her voice was warm velvet, her diction clear and perfect.

"Hi," he said, smiling eagerly at her.

The gun forgotten, he took his hand from his pocket, clasped hers briefly, and then she was past him and he closed the door. He turned to look at the back view, the straight spine, the sides curving in to the waist, blossoming below in the long curve over the hips and sweeping away down the length of leg. She was taller than he, but it didn't matter. In the rack, he'd be taller.

He wiped damp palms down the sides of his dressing gown. "You want a drink, Linda?"

"Thank you, yes." She smiled again, a warm impersonal smile, and set her purse and one glove down on an end table, then removed the other glove.

He made drinks for them both, watching her all the time, gratified by every cultured move she made, the grace of her walk across the room to the round mirror between the windows, the supple beautiful shift of curve and line as she raised her arms. She lowered her head slightly, and standing before the mirror removed the two jewel-tipped pins from her hat, took off the hat, stuck the pins back into it and set the hat down on the table by the mirror.

He watched her as they had a drink together, sitting side by side on the sofa. She turned just slightly toward him, sheathed knees together, costume and body and face and voice and speech all perfect, all meshed in wonderful symmetry, an idealization machine of flesh and blood and bone and sinew and female parts. He didn't want her now, not yet, not physically. He was content with what he had: the look of her, the presence of her, the sureness of her, the knowledge that he would have her tonight, that he had all of tonight to posses her as completely and as often as he wanted.

"I understand," she said, "that you are an executive in the organization."

He grinned. "Yeah. I'm what you might call administrative." And he found himself telling her all about his job, the responsibility it entailed, the problems hie faced, the kind of guys he had working for him.

And she responded with good questions, with an interested expression on her face, with intelligent comments. He talked on and on, knowing he was impressing her and interesting her, delighted with himself and with her, more animated and vibrant than he'd ever been before in his life. When next he looked at his watch it was seven minutes to ten.

He stopped in mid-sentence, struck by the stupidity of it. Two hours shot, gone forever, and this broad didn't even have her suit jacket off yet.

It was time. It was way past time.

But how the hell was he supposed to start? He'd spent all this time talking, and this was a high-class chick. You didn't just all of a sudden tell her to spread her legs, you had to be genteel about it. How the hell was he supposed to start?

She watched him, smiling, and said, "Is it all right if I take off my shoes? I've been wearing them for just hours."

"Yeah," he said, distracted. "Sure, go ahead."

She crossed one leg over the other, nylon brushing nylon, and removed her shoe. She was half turned toward him, and in that position he had a clear view down the length of the crossed leg, the darker band at the top of the stocking and the creamy flesh beyond.

Impulsively he reached out, stroking his hand up the underside of her leg, squeezing the top of the thigh beyond the stocking. "You're great, Linda," he said. "You're the goddam best."

She smiled again. "Help me off with my stockings, will you, Mal?"

"You bet I will."

He knelt before her, rolled the stockings down the perfect lengths of her legs. She took her jacket off and the green silk scarf and the white blouse with the lace at the throat. Her bra was white. That was better than red, he thought, looking at her—more discreet, more cultured.

She touched his jawline. "I suppose we ought to go to the bedroom now," she said softly.

"Yeah."

He followed her into the bedroom. She was barefoot, wearing gray skirt and white bra, the bra strap at the level of his chin. She asked him to unsnap her and he did, and then she stepped out of the skirt and the garter belt and the panties. He was by then out of his dressing gown and trousers and slippers, and when she lay back on the bed, arms up to enclose him, he was ready.

He should have known that a girl who could charge one hundred dollars for one night of her companionship would have to be worth it in every way. In appearance, yes. In ability to make her customer feel at ease and feel interesting and important, yes. But most of all, she would have to be worth it in bed. And she was.

Excitement and delayed expectation and her skill finished him almost at once. He lay startled and humiliated and enraged: the boy who got to the matinee just as the chapter was ending. He gnawed painfully on his lower lip, and she murmured, "That's all right, Mal. That's only warming up."

But he knew himself, he was no champion: he wasn't born to run relay races all by himself.

"Let me get up, Mal," she whispered. "I'll be right back, and don't you worry about anything."

He rolled over, and watched the grand fluidity of her body as she rose from the bed and left the room. To have had that, and only for those few seconds, that was bitter.

But when she came back, he found out at last what it truly was he was paying her for. To make him more a man than he was. With gentle smiling urgency she made him ready again, and for the second time he closed his eyes and had the time of his life. And afterwards he slept, content.

He awoke to find the nightstand lamp still burning, and her asleep beside him. The clock said twenty past three. She was lying on her back, one arm down at her side, the other bent, the hand on her stomach. Her hair was disarranged, the lipstick had been rubbed from her mouth, her body gleamed in the dim light. He looked at her now and felt only physical desire, stronger even than before.

He woke her, and she reacted at once, her arms coming around him, her body responding to him, and he just barely heard the sound of the window being raised.

He pushed up with his hands, arching his back, staring terrified over his shoulder, and saw Parker come through the window from the fire escape. His head spun around, and he saw the dressing gown on the chair beyond the nightstand. Desperately he pushed away from her, lunging headlong toward the dressing gown, knowing he would never make it.

7

Like a machine, he felt a click and it was nine months ago. At the estate, when they came back from the island and he first approached Ryan about the double cross.

"You know Parker better than I do," he'd said. "Tell me something. Would he ever try to grab the whole pie in a thing like this?"

"Parker?" Ryan shook his head. "Not a chance. I worked with him three, four times, and he's straight. Don't you worry about it."

"Okay," said Mal doubtfully. "If you say so. It's just I heard him and Sill talking, and from what they said it sounded like— it must of meant something else, that's all."

Ryan bit right away. "Wait a second. What did they say?"

"Parker said something about a two-way split. At least, that's what it sounded like. A two-way split was better, something like that. And Sill said something about you were the only guy who could fly the plane and Parker said there was still a car in the garage. The one Lynn came up in."

"Where was this?" Ryan had asked.

"When we came back, out by the plane. Remember they hung back a little?"

Ryan worried it over in his mind a minute, frowning heavily, and shook his head. "Parker's never done anything like that. Sill maybe. I don't know about him. But not Parker."

"What made me wonder," Mal said, "is because of the dough Parker needs."

"What dough?"

"Didn't you know about it? That's the whole reason he took this job, out of the country and everything. He was going to do some other job in Chicago and it fell through—"

"Yeah, yeah," said Ryan, glad to be presented with a fact he could verify. "I was in on that, too, I know about that."

"Yeah, well, Parker needs dough bad. That's why he took this job when the other one fell through. Think about it, Ryan. Did he ever work outside the country before?"

"Parker? Nah, he's always worked the states."

"That's what I mean. So I thought maybe he needed dough bad enough to want to cross us. That's why I wanted to ask your advice."

Ryan chewed on it a while longer, his head shaking slowly back and forth as he thought. Finally, he shook his head more decisively and said, "No. He wouldn't do it, Mal. He'd know better than that. I'd find him—you better believe it—and he knows that. Parker wouldn't cross me, he knows better."

"Listen, that's the part scares me. If Parker was going to cross us, he wouldn't want to leave us alive, hunting for him. He'd want to be damn sure we were dead long before he'd leave this house."

"Yeah," said Ryan slowly. "Yeah, I never thought of that."

Mal looked up at him. "What do you think we ought to do?"

"I don't know," Ryan said. "I want to think it over. Parker. It just don't sound like him."

"If he's planning anything, it'll be tonight. After we're all in bed."

"I got to think this over."

"Let me know," Mal had said. "We don't have much time!"

"Yeah. Jeez—Parker." Ryan went away shaking his head.

Later that night Mal took a knife and slit the sleeping Chester's throat. He got rid of the knife and ran to Ryan's room. "Ryan, wake up! He got Chester—Parker already done for Chester!"

Ryan hadn't been asleep. He'd been lying awake in the darkness, his hand on the gun under his pillow, his eyes watching the door. Although he hadn't said anything about it, he'd nearly shot Mal when he came into the room.

The two of them went and looked at Chester's body. "Parker," said Ryan wonderingly. He shook his head. "I wouldn't of believed it."

"We got to get him, Ryan," Mal said. "Before he gets us, we got to get him."

Ryan nodded heavily. "Yeah. I'll get the gun."

"No," said Mal. "Wait a second. We don't want to do it that way."

Ryan paused, brow furrowed. "What way, then? You got a better idea?"

Mal had a better idea. It had just come to him, just that minute, and it excited him, nerved him up, gave him goose bumps. He'd originally planned just this much, the way it was going, setting Ryan on Parker so it didn't matter which one survived. He'd be in the background waiting to finish the other.

But now all at once he had this idea, and he didn't stop to analyze it, to think about how it was more complicated, more risky, more dangerous. He just knew it was the way to do it, the way it had to be done. When things hit him that way, his mind was closed, there was no longer any possibility but the one idea strong in his head.

Lynn. Lynn Parker. The bastard's wife, the butt-twitching, high-breasted, long-legged wife.

From the minute he'd seen her first, in the cab in Chicago when he recognized Parker and braced him for the proposition, he'd had hot pants for that bitch. He'd looked at her, and wanted her, and because she was Parker's he couldn't go near her. And that made him want her all the more.

She'd do the job for them. She herself, she'd do it. It came to him, and he knew it was perfect.

"Lynn," he said. "She does the job for us. It's perfect."

Ryan frowned ponderously. "Lynn? She's his wife, Mal."

"I know that. She's the only one could catch him off guard. You know the bastard, Ryan. You want to brace him with him ready and eager for you? The hell with that."

"How you gonna get Lynn to do it? It don't make sense, Mal."

"We tell her the score. She either takes care of him or she's dead. We put it to her that way. We let her know we mean it—it's her or him."

Ryan thought slowly into it, a worried expression on his face. "I don't know, Mal," he said laboriously. "Lynn, she's his wife, I don't know—"

"You don't want to brace him, Ryan."

"Yeah. Yeah."

"It's worth a try. If it don't work, we regroup, that's all."

Ryan frowned harder.

"We don't have a hell of a lot of time," Mal said quickly. "We've got to make our move before he makes his."

"Yeah," said Ryan. "Okay. We try it."

On the way down the hall, Ryan stopped off in Sill's room for a minute. That left only Parker to be taken care of.

There was a bathroom between each pair of bedrooms, connected on both sides. They went into the bedroom next to the one occupied by Parker and Lynn, and waited by the slightly open bathroom door.

She finally came through the door on the other side, nude, and they grabbed her the minute she closed the door, and hustled her into the other bedroom. Ryan showed her the knife, darkly smeared, and Mal his gun, and she knew better than to shout.

"We got something to tell you," Mal said, talking low and quick. "Listen close. Somebody's going to die in the room next door tonight, and you got the choice. It can be you, or it can be Parker. If you want, it can be both. Which is it?"

She stared up at him, shaking her head. "I don't know what you mean. What is it, Mal? I don't know what you mean."

"I told you," he said. "Somebody's going to die in there. It's you or Parker. Take your pick."

"How can I—? I don't get it, Mal. Please, I don't know what you mean."

"Ryan, touch her with the knife," Mal said.

He touched her, the tip of the knife against the underpart of her left breast, not quite enough pressure to break the skin. Her face was big and blank.

"Take your pick, Lynn," Mal said. "You or Parker. Quick."

She licked her lips, staring from face to face. Finally, in a voice almost too low to hear, she whispered, "I don't want to die."

Mal had Sill's automatic in his pocket. He took it out and handed her his own revolver. "Point that at either Ryan or me," he said, "and you're dead right now."

She looked from the gun in her hand to his face and back to the gun again. "You want me—? You want me to—?"

"Think it over," he said. "Take your time." He ostentatiously looked at his wrist watch. "You got thirty seconds."

"You can't want *me* to—to—"

"You got twenty seconds."

"Mal, please. For God's sake, Mal—"

"Twenty seconds. Ryan, touch her with the knife again."

Ryan touched the tip of the knife to the same place on the underpart of her breast, but Mal said, "No, not there. On the red." She flinched, and he said, "Ten seconds. Yes or no?"

"Oh, God," she whispered. The knife was against her and she was afraid to move. "Don't make me kill him, Mal."

"Four seconds," he said. "Better poke a littler harder, Ryan. Two seconds. One—"

"All right!"

Mal exhaled, letting the burden slip from his shoulders. He hadn't wanted her dead. That was the last thing in the world he wanted.

It was working out fine, detail after detail, he was getting everything he wanted. He wanted the dough, all of it, to repay the syndicate and get back into the Outfit, where he belonged.

He was getting the dough, share after share, first Chester's and then Sill's and now Parker's and soon Ryan's. And he wanted Lynn, who was tied completely to Parker and he was going to get her too.

She was going to help him murder her husband, and that would be the tie between them that would bind her to him. Knowing that she could have chosen death, but had not, she would have to realize how faint her love for Parker really had been, and she would need someone who could share that knowledge and still want her. And that would be him, Mal, the one who had done it with her, the one for whom she had killed.

But it wasn't done yet. He explained to her now. He and Ryan would be in the connecting bathroom, waiting. They didn't demand that she do the job right away. She could take all the time she needed, she could wait for just the right moment. But Parker was not to leave the room alive. If he did, one second later she would be dead.

And if she tried to warn Parker, Mal and Ryan would know. They would be watching, they would be listening; they would know. One wrong word and she and Parker would die together, at the same moment. He explained it all twice, making sure she understood. She watched him dully, watching his moving lips rather than his eyes.

"All right," she said, when he was finished. "I'll do it. I told you I'd do it."

"Good."

He wanted to reach out and pat her shoulder, just touch her flesh, but some instinct warned him not to.

She crossed through the bathroom to the room where Parker lay waiting for her. She walked diagonally across to him, the gun out of his sight in her right hand, held down against her thigh. When she bent to join him, she managed to slip the gun under the mattress, and then his arms were around her and the fierce strength was on him again.

Mal stood in the bathroom, one eye closed, watching through the slit between door and jamb. The bodies moved on the bed in the dim light, and he watched, in a kind of suspended animation, waiting for the thing to be done and over with, for him to be dead and her to be his.

Ryan tugged at his arm, motioning him into the other bedroom and, irritated, he obeyed. Whispering, Ryan wanted to know why they didn't just plug Parker now, from the bathroom doorway.

Mal shook his head in exasperation. "It might kill her, too," he said. "And I want her."

Ryan said, "But she don't want you, Mal."

"She will," he said, and went back to his post at the door.

They were like something in a jungle, those two. He watched, and he couldn't believe she was always that demanding. She was giving her husband a grand send-off. Or maybe it was just that she was aware Mal was watching, that she was trying to show him how good she was.

It went on and on, until finally Parker got up from the bed and reached for his clothes. He put on a shirt and trousers, that was all, and picked up the automatic from the nightstand. Mal heard him say, "I'll go see Mal now."

Mal and Ryan exchanged glances. For Ryan, it was another confirmation of what Mal had already told him. For Mal, it was the startled realization that he'd been telling Ryan the truth all along. The son of a bitch really was planning to kill him!

They saw Parker start for the door; they saw Lynn glance over at them, her face frightened and indecisive. Mal pulled the door open an inch more, enough for her to see the automatic in his hand, and then she reached under the mattress and came up with the revolver and spoke Parker's name.

They saw the first shot catch him in the gut, and they saw her fire five more shots into him in blind panic and throw the gun away, crying out without words. And then they came into the room.

Mal sent Ryan to the garage for gasoline. They'd burn the house, get rid of all the evidence.

He told Lynn to get dressed. He'd planned to take her now, for the first time, right here in the same room with her dead husband, but the look on her face stopped him. Besides, he felt a sudden urgent need to be out of here, to have the thing behind him and finished and in the past.

They fired the house and left, and on the way to the plane he shot Ryan in the back. "I can fly a plane too," he told her, grinning. "He never knew that. I'm smarter than Parker thought."

In the plane, he told her why he was justified. "Parker was figuring to kill me, wasn't he? It was him or me. Just like it was him or you. The same thing."

She answered only when he demanded an answer, and then only in monosyllables.

He got to her the first time in Chicago.

He'd gone to the Outfit and he'd given them the money, and they'd just stared at him. They couldn't believe it. "We'll let you know, Mal," they'd said. "We'll give you a call in a couple days."

So he went back to the hotel, where she sat waiting for him because there was no place else for her to go, and he got to her for the first time. And she just lay there. He beat upon her like the waves upon a rocky cliff, and like a rocky cliff she remained unmoved. Her expression was dull, her body was unresponsive, her emotions were away off somewhere.

So he figured it was just that it was too soon, she needed some time to adjust. She hadn't argued about his right to take her; there really wasn't any problem. She'd come out of it soon enough.

Two days later, a guy came around from the Outfit. He was impressed by the suite, that was clear enough, and he was impressed by the quality of the woman Mal had there with him. And the Outfit was already impressed by the money he'd paid them.

A guy who had the guts to go out and grab that kind of dough, and the loyalty to use it to repay a debt to the Outfit, was a guy the Outfit could use. They had a slot for him. If he worked out this time, he had it made.

There was only one small thing. It would be best if he didn't work in Chicago. A lot of the rank and file in Chicago knew about his blunder: it might make it difficult for him to be an effective administrator. They had a slot for him in New York.

That was fine by Mal. He wasn't particularly hipped on Chicago anyway. He thought he'd like New York.

Lynn went with him. She had nowhere else to go.

In New York they made him a sales manager, liquor division. Cigarettes are cheap in the District of Columbia. There's no state sales tax. Cigarettes are expensive in Canada. There's an import duty on American brands. On the other hand, Canadian whiskey is cheap in Canada, but there's an import duty making it expensive in the United States.

So the cars full of cigarettes drive north from Washington, and the same cars, now full of whiskey, drive south from Montreal. About half of the liquor cargo goes as far as New York, and the rest goes on down to Washington.

Mal was the guy who received the liquor shipments in New York. He managed the crew that sold the stuff to selected restaurants and bars and liquor stores. It was purely administrative, seeing that the right quantities went to the right places at the right times, and that nobody tapped the take. It was a job he could do, a job he could like. He fitted in well.

And Lynn stayed with him. She had nowhere else to go. But she didn't warm up, no matter what he tried, no matter how much time he spent with her, no matter how much dough he spent on her, no matter what. She was a large-as-life doll, no more. It was as though his sweating hulking panting body weren't even there.

He took to getting his satisfaction elsewhere, with Pearl and with others. He moved out completely at last, giving her enough dough to support herself, and she stayed because she had nowhere else to go. It had occurred to him finally to be afraid of her, to realize that she might one day decide, in desperate expiation, to kill him as she had killed Parker. So when he moved out he made sure she couldn't find him. She didn't object; she didn't suppose that she'd ever want to find him for anything.

The time went by and he settled into his life, getting used to the job and the people and the city, knowing that he was doing good work and that he would within a year or two be in line for a boost up the ladder. Keeley's Island and the estate and the eighty thousand dollars gradually faded into memory, until a guy named Stegman told him that Parker was alive and looking.

The dead man fulfilled his ambitions. He got the best hotel suite and the best professional lay. And he got them just in time.

THREE

1

*F*or Parker, it had been a cold thin trail from Stegman the cab-man in Canarsie to the window of the St. David Hotel. The Canarsie thing had been a dead end. Lynn had been easy to find; she'd had a telephone listing under her own name. No reason for her not to—Parker was supposed to be dead. But Mal was more cautious. Or he was using a different name.

So Parker had come back to Manhattan from Canarsie, to the hotel where they'd kept the room for him because he hadn't told them otherwise. He'd stripped off the clothing he'd worn for the last three days, showered and shaved, dressed again, and gone out for something to eat, and to think it over. . . .

Sitting at the table in the restaurant, he'd worked it out in his mind. He'd tried to get to Mal through Lynn, and the trail had gone cold almost before it started. So now he'd have to try it a different way. Mal was supposed to be connected with the syndicate again. Maybe he could find him through the syndicate.

He didn't like it that way. Syndicate people had a reputation for sticking together. He'd start nosing around and, the first thing, Mal would hear about it. Mal would know he was alive and looking for him. But it ought to flush him out. And otherwise the whole thing was hung up, no place to go.

He finished his meal and took a cab uptown to Central Park West and 104th Street. This was the wrong end of the park where the slums had spread south and east to lap at the very edge of the greenery. Parker walked west on 104th till he came to the grocery store. BODEGA, it called itself, Spanish for grocery, in black letters on yellow, beneath the Pepsi-Cola emblem. Underneath BODEGA it gave the proprietor's name in smaller black letters. *Delgardo.*

Inside there was a stink compounded of roach poison, rotted flour, floor wax, old wood, humankind and a hundred other things. Two short heavy women in shiny black fingered the hard rolls. In the narrow space behind the counter a tiny fat man with a thick moustache scratched his left elbow and looked at nothing at all.

Parker pushed past the women and said to the man, "Is Jimmy around these days?"

Delgardo kept scratching his elbow. His eyes came back from infinity and studied Parker's face. "You a friend of Jimmy's?"

"Yeah."

"So how come you don't know where he is?"

"We lost touch."

"So how come I never seen you before?"

"Jimmy drove for me on that payroll job in Buffalo."

Delgardo's hands twitched suddenly, and his eyes flicked in alarm to the two women. In a quick undertone he said, "Don't talk that way."

Without lowering his voice Parker said, "You wanted to know

who I was. Now you know. Now you can tell me where Jimmy is."

Delgardo fidgeted a minute, but the two women had shown no signs of interest. He fingered his mustache nervously and said, "Come in the back."

Parker followed him deeper into the store, past a greasy curtain. In the back room the stink was even stronger. Delgardo, smelling of peppers, came close to whisper, "He's in Canada. Driving, you know."

"Cigarettes?"

"Yes."

"When's he coming back?"

"Two, three days."

"Gimme pencil and paper."

"Yes. Wait here."

Parker waited, lighting a cigarette against the stink, while Delgardo went back to the front of the store. There was a flurry of rapid-fire Spanish between Delgardo and one or both of the women. They'd been stealing while he was in back.

He came back angry, and took a deep breath. He shrugged at Parker. "You know how they are."

He gave him a long yellow pencil and a greasy three-by-five memo pad and Parker wrote down the name of the hotel.

"When he comes back, he should call me there. Parker, tell him. If I'm not in, leave a message."

"Parker? You better write it down."

"It's an easy name to remember."

Parker gave him back the memo pad and pencil. Delgardo hesitated, still wanting him to write the name down, then shrugged and led the way back to the front of the store.

The two women were still there, looking silent and frightened. Two uniformed policemen were there, too, filling the store. Their expressions blank and hard, they studied Parker, and Parker said, "Wallet." He reached slowly to his back pocket. They waited, and Parker pulled out the wallet and handed it to the nearest of them.

They both read the driver's license, giving his name as Edward Johnson, and then they gave the wallet back and one of them said, "What was the business in the back of the store? Did you buy something or sell something?"

"Neither."

"Nothing like that, officers," said Delgardo hurriedly. "You know me, I don't do nothing like that." He was sweating beneath his mustache.

"Nothing like what?" one of the cops asked.

Delgardo looked flustered. Parker said, "Nothing like junk." He shucked off his jacket, rolled up his shirt sleeves, showed them his bare arms. "I don't take it, buy it, sell it or carry it," he said. "Get the broads out of here, I'll show you my legs. No needle marks there either."

"That won't be necessary," said the talking cop. "Just empty your pockets. You too, Delgardo. And let's see the pad."

He glanced at the memo pad, looked at Parker. "What's doing at the Carlington Hotel?"

"I'm staying there," Parker said.

"That isn't what it said on your driver's license."

"I had a fight with my wife."

"What was the business in the back of the store?"

"We had a Coke together," said Parker. "I'm an old friend of Jimmy's. I come around to look him up."

"An old friend from where?"

"Upstate. We worked for the same trucker, up in Buffalo."

"How come you don't have a chauffeur's license?"

"I don't do that kind of work any more."

"What kind of work do you do now?"

"I'm unemployed. I was laid off. That's what the fight was all about."

"What fight?"

"With my wife. I told you."

"Laid off from where?"

"General Electric. Out on the Island."

The cop chewed the inside of his cheek a minute, and glanced at his partner. "You tell a good story, Johnson. But you feel wrong."

Parker shrugged.

The cop said, "How come you're so hipped on narcotics? How come you brought the subject up the minute you saw us?"

"The neighborhood has a reputation," Parker said. "I been reading the *Post*."

"Yeah. Lean up against the wall there."

Parker leaned forward, palms flat against the wall, and the cop frisked him briefly, then stepped back, saying, "Okay."

"I'm clean," Parker said. "Do I take my goods back now?"

"Yes."

Parker took his wallet and change and cigarettes from the counter top and put them back in his pocket, watching as Delgardo was frisked and also found clean. The talking cop nodded sourly at Parker and said, "You can go. I suppose we'll be seeing you around."

"I doubt it," Parker said. "It's more civilized downtown."

"We didn't ask for this precinct," the cop said.

"Nobody did," Parker said.

"Take off," said the other cop.

Parker went on out, pushing past the two women, who still look terrified. They hadn't understood a word. They believed Delgardo had called the police to arrest them for shoplifting.

2

"*I*'m looking for a girl," said Parker.

She smirked at him. "What do you think I am, big boy—a watermelon?"

Parker picked up his beer glass, looking at the cool wet ring it left on the bar. "I'm looking for a particular girl," he said.

She arched a brow. She plucked her eyebrows and painted on new ones, in the wrong place, so that when she arched a brow it came out wrong, like a badly animated cartoon. "A hustler? I don't know them all, baby."

"She'd work by telephone," he said. "She wouldn't be a loner, she'd be connected with the organization."

She shook her head. "Then I wouldn't know her."

Parker emptied the glass, motioned at the bartender for another round. "You'd know people who might know her," he said.

"I might and I might not." The round came and she said, "Thanks. Why should I tell you anything? I don't know you from Adam."

He looked at her. "Do I look like law?"

She laughed. "Not much. That's one thing you're not. But maybe you want to give her a bad time. Maybe she gave you athlete's foot once or something."

"I'm her brother," Parker lied. "We been out of touch. The doctor tells me I got a little cancer in my throat. I want to look her up, you know how it is. It's my last chance."

She looked shocked and mournful. "Jeez," she said. "That's a bitch, man. I'm sorry."

Parker shrugged. "I had a good life. I got maybe six months to go. So I thought I'd look her up. There's just her and this aunt of ours, and I wouldn't look the aunt up if she had a cancer cure."

"Jeez," she said again. Meditations on mortality creased her brow. "I know how you feel, man," she said. "You maybe don't think so, but I do. In this lousy business, you got to be thinking about disease all the time. There was this girl I knew, we used to room together. She didn't feel so good, and it hurt to swallow, and sometimes she'd spit blood, so she thought it was TB. I told her and told her, go down to the clinic, so finally she did, and they put her in the hospital. She had a little something in the back of her throat too. Not cancer. The occupational disease, you know?"

Parker nodded. He couldn't care less, but if he let her talk about this maybe she'd talk about the other.

"She's still in there," she said. "I went to see her once, and it was awful. She looked like an old bag, you know? And she couldn't even talk any more, just croak. That was about six months ago, I went to see her. And that was enough for me, brother, I didn't go back since. For all I know, she's dead by now.

She'd be better off." Then she caught herself, and went wide-eyed, clapping a hand over her mouth.

"That's okay," Parker said. "I know what you mean. Me, I figure I'm not going to stick around for that part. When it gets too bad, I slit this vein here." He turned his hand over, showing the wrist. "See? That blue one there."

She shivered. "Don't talk that way, will you, baby? You get me all depressed."

"Sorry." Parker swallowed half his beer. "About my sister," he said.

"What's her name? You never know, I might know her."

"The last I heard, she was calling herself Rose Leigh."

She thought, brows furrowing in the wrong places. Shaking her head, she said, "No, I don't think so. For a minute it sounded kind of familiar, but I guess not."

"It's from the old song," he said. "Rosalie, my darling, Rosalie, my love— That's why it sounds familiar."

"That must be it. Listen, Bernie might know her."

"Bernie?"

"The barman. They sometimes take calls in here." She raised a hand. "Hey, Bernie!"

He came down along the boards behind the bar, expressionless. "Another round?"

"In a minute," she said. She leaned over the bar toward him, urgent and intent. "Listen, Bernie, do you know a hustler named Rose Leigh? Like the song?"

"Rose?" He shrugged. "Not to look at, no. She never come in here at all. But I know the name, yeah. From the phone."

"This is her brother," she said, stabbing a purple-nailed thumb at Parker. "He's looking for her."

Bernie studied Parker dispassionately. "To take her home?"

Parker shook his head. "We been out of touch. I want to look her up is all."

"He's sick," she said, in a loud stage whisper. "He wants to see his sister again, you know?"

Bernie wasn't a sentimentalist. He said, "So what do you want from me?"

"Where does he find her?"

"How should I know? I know the name only from the phone."

"Where do I find somebody who knows where she is?" Parker asked him.

Bernie thought it over. "I don't know you, buddy," he said at last. "I wouldn't want to tell you something I shouldn't."

She opened her big mouth again. "Maybe you could call to somebody to tell her her brother's in town."

Bernie liked that. "Yeah," he said. "That I can do for you."

"Have them tell her it's Parker. That way she'll know it's really me."

Bernie nodded. He went away and she said, "You came to the right place, mister. Bernie can help you out."

"I came where the hustlers were," he said.

"Speaking of that, I still got to make a buck. I'd like to stick around and talk with you but—"

"That's all right."

"Good luck," she said.

"Thanks."

She climbed down off the stool, tugging her skirt down over thick hips, and promenaded toward the door. Halfway there, she caught a high sign and angled instead over to a table where two guys were sitting across from one another, looking eager.

She stood at the table, talking with them a minute, then went back and talked to a girl sitting at the end of the bar. The other girl studied the two guys, then nodded and they both went back to the table.

Parker watched it all in the back mirror. The four of them, now two couples, were just getting up from the table when Bernie came back from the pay phone. "They'll call back in a little while."

"You told them Parker?"

"Yeah."

"Fine. Thanks." He pushed his empty glass forward. "Another of these."

He waited twenty-five minutes. If this fell through, if he couldn't find her or she couldn't find out where Mal was, he'd have to wait for Jimmy Delgardo. And if Jimmy didn't work out either, he'd have to try some completely different way. It didn't matter. He had all the time in the world. Mal, the fat cat. What back fence are you sitting on, Mal?

When the phone in the pay booth rang, he watched Bernie walk slowly and deliberately down the length of the bar, lift the hinged flap at the end and step through, close the flap after himself, step into the booth and close the door. He picked up the phone and spoke, and listened. Then he looked at Parker, and they looked at each other as he spoke again. Giving a description.

Finally, he put the receiver down on the shelf and opened the door. "It's for you."

Parker went back and into the phone booth, shutting the door. It was hot in there. Before picking up the receiver, he clicked on the fan. It whirred, and blew air past his neck.

He said, "Hello."

A girl's voice said, "Okay, smart boy, who are you?"

"Hi, Wanda," he said.

"The name is Rose."

"It used to be Wanda. This is Parker, like the man said."

"Try again, smart boy. Parker's dead."

"I know it. But I couldn't rest easy till I paid you the twenty bucks."

The line hummed in his ear for a few seconds, and then she said, "Is it really Parker?"

"I told you it was."

"But—I saw Lynn in Stern's, three, four months ago. She said you was dead."

"She thought I was. I want to talk to you."

"You're lucky," she said. "This is my monthly vacation. 298 West 65th—the name is by the bell downstairs."

"I'll be right there."

"Wait. Let me talk to the bartender again. I'm supposed to tell him whether you're straight or not."

"Sure."

He went out of the phone booth, and it suddenly seemed a lot cooler in the bar. He caught Bernie's eye, and motioned at the phone. "She wants to talk to you again."

Bernie nodded and came back down the bar. On the way by he said, "Stick around a minute, huh?"

Parker nodded. Two guys down at the end of the bar by the door were definitely not looking at him.

Bernie talked briefly on the phone, then hung up and came back. A smile worked its way lugubriously up out of his gut, fading away when it reached his face. "Okay, friend," he said. "Glad I could help you."

"Thanks again," said Parker. He got off the stool and headed for the door. The two guys at the end of the bar looked at him now.

3

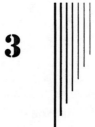

*S*he hadn't changed. She still looked seventeen, though by now she must be pushing thirty-five. Her smallness helped; she was barely five feet tall and delicately boned. Her eyes were large and round and green, her hair was flaming red, her rosebud mouth was a carmine blossom against a pale clear complexion.

Her body was beautifully proportioned for her size, with conical well-separated breasts, a fragile waist, low-slung hips. Only her speech gave her away: it was not the speech of a college freshman.

She flung open the door, wearing a swirling muumuu with at least ten colors on it, and cried, "Come on in here, you lovely bastard—let me welcome you back to life."

He nodded, and brushed past her through the foyer and down the two steps into a huge movie set of a living room. Porcelain figures, mostly of frogs, crammed all the table tops.

"Surly Parker," she said, closing the door and coming down the steps after him. "You're the same as ever."

"So are you. I want to ask you a favor."

"I thought you were my long lost brother. Sit down. What are you drinking?"

"I'll take a beer."

"I've got vodka."

"Beer."

"Oh well, the hell with it. I should have known better. Parker doesn't make social calls. You don't have to have the beer if you don't want it."

"Good," he said. He sat down on the sofa. "You look good."

She sat on the leather chair facing him, flouncing into it, one leg dangling over the arm. "Small talk was never your forte," she said. "Go ahead and ask your favor."

"You know a guy named Mal Resnick?"

She hunched her shoulders, bit the corner of her lower lip, stared sideways at a fringed lampshade. "Resnick," she said, the name coming out muffled because her teeth still held the corner of her lip. "Resnick." Then she shook her head and bounced to her feet. "Nope, it doesn't ring a bell. Was he one of our crowd? Should I know him from the coast?"

"No, from here in New York. He's in the syndicate somewhere."

"The *Outfit,* baby. We don't say syndicate any more. It's square."

"I don't care what you call it."

"Anyway—oh." Her eyes widened and she stared at the ceiling. "Oh! *That* bastard!"

"You know him?"

"No, *of* him. One of the girls was bitching to me. He got her for an all night—it was supposed to be fifty bucks. There was only thirty-five in the envelope. She complained to Irma, and

Irma told her there was no sense raising a stink about it, he was in the Outfit. She said he was lousy anyway. All grunts and groans, no real action."

Parker leaned forward, elbows on knees, and cracked his knuckles. "You can find out where he is?"

"I suppose he's at the Outfit," she said.

"What's that, some kind of club?"

"No, the hotel." She started to say more, then suddenly swirled around, reaching for a carved silver box on the teakwood table. She flipped it open, withdrew a cigarette with a rose red filter, and picked up a heavy silver Grecian-style lighter.

Parker watched her, waiting till she had the cigarette lit before he said, "Okay, Wanda, what is it?"

"Call me Rose, will you, dear? I'm out of the habit of answering to the other."

"What is it?"

She looked at him a moment, thoughtfully, cigarette smoke misting around her face. Then she nodded and said, "We're friends, Parker. I suppose we're friends, if either one of us could be said to have friends."

"That's why I came to you."

"Sure. The loyalty of friendship. But I'm an employee, too, Parker. In a business where it pays to have loyalty to the company. And the company wouldn't like me to tell anybody about the Outfit hotel."

"So you didn't tell me a thing." He cracked his knuckles impatiently. "You know that already, why talk about it?"

"How strong are you, Parker?" She turned away and walked across the room to the draped windows, talking over her shoulder as she went. "I've often wondered about that. I think you're the strongest man I've ever met." She stopped and looked back at him, one hand on the drapes. "But I wonder if that's enough."

"Enough for what?"

She pulled the drape to one side. The window was tall and wide. She stood framed against it, looking out, tiny and shapely. "You want an Outfit man named Resnick," she said. "If I know you, you want him for something he won't like."

"I'm going to kill him," Parker said.

She smiled, nodding. "There," she said. "That's something he won't like. But what if something goes wrong, and you get grabbed, and they ask you where you found out about the hotel? If they ask you hard?"

"I got it from a guy named Stegman."

"Oh? What you got against Stegman?"

"Nothing, it's just believable. Why, do you know him?"

"No." She slid the drapes shut again, prowled the room some more, crossing to the opposite side merely to flick ashes into a blue seashell. "All right," she said, "you wait here. I'll make a phone call. I want to know for sure whether that's where he is or not."

"Fine."

"If you want a beer after all," she said, "the kitchen is that way."

She left the room, and he killed time by lighting a cigarette. Then he picked up a green porcelain frog from the nearest table and looked at it. It gleamed and its eyes were black. He turned it over and it was hollow, with a round hole in the bottom, and the words *Made in Japan* impressed in the porcelain next to the hole. He put the frog back and looked around at the room. She was doing all right these days.

She came back and said, "He's there. I even got the room number."

"Fine," he said, getting to his feet.

She smiled, with a trace of sourness. "You aren't a guy for small talk," she said. "Get what you want, and go."

"One thing at a time," he said, "that's all I can think about. Maybe I'll come back and see you later?"

"The hell you will. Here, I wrote it down."

He took the paper from her and read her small careful script—Oakwood Arms, Park Avenue and 57th Street. Suite 361. He read it three times, then crumpled the paper and dropped it into a free-form glass ashtray. "Thanks."

"Anytime, dear heart. We're friends, aren't we?" The sarcasm twisted her mouth.

He reached into his pocket, dragged out his wallet. "I meant it about the twenty bucks," he said.

She looked at the two tens he held out to her, hesitating.

"Oh, go to hell, will you? Get yourself killed, you bastard. Seven years, and you don't even ask me how I've been."

Parker put the tens back in the wallet, the wallet back in his pocket. "The next time," he said, "I'll bring slides."

She snatched up a frog, spun around to hurl it at him, and stopped. He stood waiting, looking at her. Her arm dropped. She muttered, "I ought to tell him you're coming."

"You don't want to do that," he said. He walked to the door.

4

*T*he waitress kept asking him if he wanted anything else.

It distracted him from looking out at the street. She had a band on her finger, so finally he said, "What's the matter, don't you get enough from your husband?" So after that she left him alone.

She glared awhile from the other end of the counter, but he could ignore that. He could look out at the street, and let his fifteen-cent cup of coffee cool. It was a Park Avenue coffee shop, and expensive. Pastrami on rye, eighty-five cents, no butter. Like that.

Directly across the street was the Oakwood Arms, a gray stone hulk with a modest marquee. A thin tall white-haired guy worked the front steps with a yellow-handled broom for a while, then went back inside. He and the doorman were both in blue uniforms with yellow trim.

A cab pulled up and two hefty matrons got out, giggling at each other as they pawed through their pocketbooks to pay the cabby. A blue-uniformed bellboy trotted through the revolving door and down the clean steps and the cabby opened the trunk. One matron had light blue luggage, the other light gray.

The cabby drove away, with a fifteen percent tip on the button, and as the matrons and bellboys were going in a guy in a pale gray suit came out, looking prosperous, followed by a younger guy in a black suit, looking cautious. Parker watched the two of them, ticking them off in his mind. Outfit wheel and bodyguard.

The wheel flagged a cab, while the bodyguard looked all around, and then they got in and drove away.

It was getting dark now. The hell of it was, he didn't know whether Mal was out or in. If he was out, then he'd have to wait while he went in and then came back out again. If he was in, it would be simpler.

Guests arrived, most of them obvious tourists, a few obvious Outfit people, a few others borderline. None of them Mal, and none of them he recognized. Aside from himself, there was no stakeout outside the building.

But he knew what there'd be inside: two or three guys sitting around in lobby chairs, reading papers, glancing up whenever somebody came in. If the somebody was wrong, a somebody the Outfit didn't want there, the two or three guys would put down their papers and saunter over and book-end him away through a door out of the lobby. They'd take him into a back room where they could ask him what they wanted to or tell him what they wanted to tell him.

Mal had picked a good place to live. It would be tough to get in there without being spotted. To left and right of the lobby entrance were storefronts with street entrances, a cigar store to the left and a coffee shop to the right. There'd be entrances from them into the hotel, but that wasn't any good. Those entrances would be watched, too.

The waitress came back, still angry. "If you don't want anything else," she said, "let someone else sit down."

He looked down the counter. Half the stools were empty. "Another cup of coffee," he said. "This one's cold."

She was going to say something, but the owner was sitting at the cash register, looking over at them. She took the coffee cup away, brought it back refilled, and added another fifteen cents onto his check.

He was going to have to find someplace else to watch from. Next door on one side was a florist and then the corner, on the other side an antique store and a shoe store and other impossibilities all the way down to the next corner. But this place would close eventually, and the waitress irritated him.

Maybe the second floor of something. He left the new cup of coffee but no tip, paid the owner his thirty cents, and walked out to the street. Across the way, an Outfit girl got out of a cab and hip-swiveled up the steps. The doorman grinned at her and she grinned back.

Parker stood on the sidewalk, looking up at the things printed on second-story windows. A dentist, a beauty parlor, a secondhand clothing store, a stamp and coin store, another dentist. It was getting dark and the lights were out behind all the windows except the clothing store. He glanced across the street, but nothing was happening.

The door beside the coffee shop said it was the entrance to the dentist and the beauty shop. It also said there was a wig store and a lawyer on the third floor. Parker went in and up the stairs. Mal might be coming out right now, while he was on the stairs.

He went up the stairs mad and came to the landing. Dentist to the right, beauty parlor to the left, frosted glass in the upper half of the doors. There was light against the glass of the beauty parlor door. He knocked, clenching his other fist impatiently, and after a minute a shadow showed on the glass and a woman's voice called, "Who is it?"

"I've got the coffee."

After a puzzled second, she said, "What coffee? I didn't order any coffee."

"From the shop downstairs," he said. "The boss said the beauty parlor."

"But I didn't *order* any coffee."

"Lady," he said, "they give me the order for the beauty shop."

She opened the door to argue with him, a small woman with too much makeup on, and as her eyes were widening he clipped her, base-joint knuckles against the tip of her chin. Her eyes rolled back and she fell like glass.

He went in, closing the door fast, stepping over her. It was an anteroom. A gooseneck lamp lit the money on the desk. She'd been counting the day's take.

He went through the other door to the darkened room where all the machinery was, the dryers looking like big-headed praying mantises. He looked down through the word *Beauty* on the window. Nothing was happening. Maybe Mal came out while he was on the stairs. All right, he'd be back before morning.

Maybe that Outfit girl was for him. Maybe he wouldn't be going out at all. All right, all right, he had time. He had nothing but time.

In the dark, he unplugged two dryers, ripped the cords loose at the bases, carried them back to the other room. The woman hadn't moved. He used one cord to tie her hands behind her, the other to tie her ankles. He found scissors in a desk drawer next to an inhaler, snipped off part of her slip and used it for a gag. She had good legs— But not now. After it was over, after Mal was dead, he'd want somebody then.

He went back to the other room, dragged a chair over to the window, sat down and smoked. People went in, people went out.

It was a bad position. If Mal came out and flagged a cab, then what? He might have to wait a few minutes for the cab, time for Parker to get downstairs, but maybe not. If he came out and walked, that would be better. If he didn't come out at all, that would be worse.

There had to be a way in there. The hotel wasn't right on the corner. There was a slender office building next to it on that side. Another hotel on the other side. The Oakwood Arms went eleven stories, the hotel on its left only nine. The office building went twenty-some.

In from the roof? Then he'd have to get down to the third floor. He didn't like that way. But if nothing happened before two o'clock, he'd have to try it.

People went in, people came out. He recognized one guy; he'd seen him around Chicago. An Outfit man. But no Mal.

He finished his last cigarette, and that made him nervous. He didn't want to leave the window, but he did. The woman's purse was on the desk, shoved back out of the way of the money. She had half a pack of filters. He slipped them in his shirt pocket.

He looked over at her; she was still out. That bothered him. She was on her side, her face in shadow. He went over and looked more closely, and her eyes were bugged halfway out of their sockets, her throat and face bluish red and mottled. He remembered the inhaler that had been in the drawer with the scissors. She'd had sinus trouble or something like that, and her nose clogged up.

It was stupid. He didn't like it, it was stupid. There wasn't any reason for her to be dead. There wasn't any reason for a gag across the mouth to make her dead. Angry at the stupidity, he went back into the other room and sat down at the window again. He smoked the filters, but they were too mild. He couldn't taste a thing, so he dragged too deeply and smoked too frequently and his throat got sore. And it was getting close in there.

He waited and he watched. And no Mal. At two o'clock, there was one Newport left. He left it in its crush-proof box on her desk, with the money. His prints were all over everything. Ronald Casper, the vag who killed the guard out in California, had killed again. It wasn't worth it to try to wipe all the prints away. If they ever got him, the California guard would be enough. They wouldn't need this broad with congestion trouble.

He went down the stairs to the street, and into the coffee shop. They were just closing up; a colored boy was mopping the floor, the chairs were all upended on the tables.

The owner was behind the counter now, two customers sat on stools. Parker said, "A pack of Luckies, and eight coffees to go. Five regular, two with sugar, one black."

"You just made it," the owner told him. "I'm just closing up. Two o'clock—closing up."

"If you got a little cardboard box," Parker said, "it'll be easier to carry than a bag."

"Five minutes later," the owner told him, "you'd of been out of luck."

He opened the Luckies right away and lit one. Then he paid for the coffees, which were in a shallow gray cardboard box, and the owner held the door open for him.

He went diagonally across the street to the office building. If Mal came out right now, it would be another stupidity. He would see Parker, and duck back inside and stay there. And make the whole thing tougher.

But Mal didn't come out. And the office building on the corner was open twenty-four hours. That meant there was an employee on all night to run the elevator and open and shut the door for late-working tenants. Watching from the beauty shop window, Parker had seen three men come out of there a little after midnight and the employee lock up again after them. And on a few floors there were still lights on.

There were four glass doors in a row. Looking through them, he could see two elevators and a guy in a gray uniform sitting on a kitchen chair beside a wooden podium with a sign-in book on it. The guy was reading the *News*.

Parker kicked the door down at the bottom where the metal was, and the guy put down his *News* and strolled across the shiny geometric floor. He studied Parker and then noticed the carton of coffee, then nodded and knelt on one knee to unlock the door. The lock was down next to the floor in the metal strip along the bottom of the door.

Parker went in, and the employee locked the door again. He straightened arthritically and said, "Nice night."

"Uh huh."

They went back to the elevators. Both were at ground floor, but only one had a light on inside. They got into that one and Parker said, "Twelve."

"Right."

On the way up, the operator wanted to know if Parker had read that thing in the paper about them two kids, and Parker said no he hadn't. They got to the twelfth floor and he said, "You want me to wait?"

"No," Parker said. "I got five here, and three on the tenth. I can walk down to the tenth and then I'll buzz you."

"Okay by me."

The doors slid shut, and Parker dropped the carton, not caring where it went. It hit the floor and the coffee containers rolled and spilled, making a mess. He went down to the end of the corridor, turned right and came to a door with lettering on it about accountants. He took off his shoe and smashed a hole in the frosted glass near the knob. Then he put his shoe back on, reached through the hole and unlocked the door.

There were air conditioners in all the windows. Looking out over one of them, he could see the hotel roof half a floor down, six or seven feet. An easy jump.

He knocked out the glass over the air conditioner and climbed through, dropping onto the hotel roof. Ahead of him was the door to the stairs. He went over and tried it; it was locked, the way he'd expected, so he went over to the edge of the roof overlooking the rear wall where the fire escape was. The back of another building was crowded in close, and down between them was utter blackness.

The first part of the fire escape was a metal ladder, down to the top floor landing. The window there was wide and low-silled, and opened into the hallway. The hall was dimly lit and empty, but the window was locked.

He went back up the fire escape and over the roof again and

up through the window into the accountants' office. He searched through drawers, and in a kind of big closet full of supplies and a mimeograph machine he found a large screwdriver and a hammer and an uninked stamp pad. He took these and went back out and across the roof and down to the window. It would be easier just to break the window, but he didn't want any noise.

He shoved the screwdriver up into the crack between the two parts of the window, by the lock. Then he took the soft pad out of its metal box and held it against the top part of the screwdriver to muffle the sound when he hit it with the hammer.

The screwdriver went in slowly, spreading the two parts of the window apart, straining the lock until finally it snapped. Then the screwdriver fell out, clattering against the metal of the fire escape, and he hunched unbreathing by the window after he retrieved it until he was sure no one had heard the sound.

He pushed the window up, climbed through, slid the window closed again. The red bulb over the window stained his face and hands with color.

He found the stairs and went down them quickly, pausing at each landing to listen. He met no one, and at the third floor he stood for a long moment at the door before cautiously pulling it open.

The hall was empty.

He found 361 around to the right. It was easy to get in—the screwdriver slipped between door and jamb with no trouble, clicking back the tumbler.

He went in cautiously, alert for any sound, any movement. The suite was dark. Not home, or asleep? He went across the living room in the darkness, grateful for the quiet thickness of the rug, and looked through the bedroom door.

The bed was empty and unmade—no sheets, no blankets, no pillow. The mattress was striped gray and white, shining dimly in the faint light from the window.

Startled, he went into the room, looked around and hurried over to the closet and pulled the door open.

It was empty. Nobody lived here any more.

5

As she was turning the knob, he shoved against the door, knocking her backward. She nearly fell down the three steps into the living room, but caught her balance just in time. He pushed into the apartment, angry and hard, slamming the door behind him.

"He's moved," he said. "The bastard moved out."

"You almost knocked me down the steps," she said. She was wearing a pale blue silk robe now, and slippers with blue puffs. In the living room, the late movie was finishing on television.

"He's moved out, I told you. Clothes, everything. Nobody lives in that damn room."

She heard him that time. "Mal?"

"Who else would I be talking about? Wanda, you better come straight with me."

"Call me Rose," she said automatically. "I'm not used to answering to the other name any more."

"I don't care what you're used to, Wanda." Parker advanced on her, grim faced, and she backed down the steps into the living room. Her face was at the level of his chest. He reached out a hand and grabbed her by the hair, twisting his hand in it and pulling her close. "He isn't there," he said, "and I want you to tell me, Wanda. Was he ever there?"

"Parker, I swear to you—" She was terrified now, knowing him from old times, and she was babbling. "I swear to you, I swear—"

"He isn't there, Wanda," he said again, as though she hadn't yet understood him. "The bed isn't made, the closet is empty, there's nothing around that belongs to anybody. He isn't there, and I want to know if he ever was there."

"Parker, Puh-Parker—" His hand twisted in her hair, and she stood on tiptoe, trying to stop the pain. "I wouldn't lie to you," she babbled. "I wouldn't have any reason to lie to you."

"One reason," he said. He twisted harder, lifted her higher so her toes barely touched the floor. "If you thought maybe you had a grudge against me, Wanda, that could be a reason. Send me to the Outfit hotel, let me barge in looking for a guy who isn't there, let the Outfit grab me and take care of me. That could be a reason."

"No grudge, Parker!" she cried. "I don't have any grudge— what grudge could I have against you?"

"You tell me, Wanda."

"Parker, please!"

He let her go so suddenly she lost her balance and fell to the floor. Her red hair was a tangle around her face. She looked up at him, not knowing what he was going to do next, and he said, "For just a little while, Wanda, I'm going to believe you. For just a little while. I'm going to believe that Mal used to live in that room, and that for some reason he moved out. He got spooked or something and—"

He stopped, raising his eyes from her to look across the room at the draped window. "Spooked," he said again. "Maybe. Found out about me maybe. Gone into a hole somewhere."

"He lived there, Parker," she said desperately. "The girl he underpaid, she gave me the address. That's the honest-to-God truth, Parker—I swear it."

"Oh, Mal," he said. "Oh, you bastard." Then his head came down, he stared at her again, still asprawl on the floor. "You find out where, Wanda. You find out where he's run to."

"How can I? Parker, for God's sake, be reasonable. How *can* I?"

"I know that bastard," he said. "He went running into his hole, thinking about me and death. And he called up for a girl, Wanda, you can bet on it. I know that little bastard; he called for a girl. You call the same place, Wanda, and you find out where."

"How can I?" Sitting rumpled on the floor, she spread her arms in an exaggerated gesture. "What reason can I give? I can't just call up, Parker—they'll want to know why."

"All right," he said. "You loaned him twenty bucks. You met at a party or something, and you loaned him twenty bucks. He was supposed to pay it back today, so you went over to the hotel and he'd moved out. And you want to know where he is now, so you can go over tomorrow and get your dough back. You got that?"

"Parker, I don't know—"

"You better know. Get on your feet."

She'd shifted position, the robe falling open below the sash at the waist, and her legs were tanned while her belly was white, and it reminded him of Lynn, that last night when he'd gone to her apartment. He turned away, irritated, saying, "Fix your robe. Get to your feet."

She got up shakily, eyeing him apprehensively, terrified of him in this mood, not knowing what else he would demand of her. "I'll try," she said, wanting to placate him. "I'll try, Parker, I'll do my best."

"That's good," he said.

He followed her into the bedroom where the phone was. There was a king-sized bed with a satiny blue spread, and a cream-painted night table. The phone was on the nightstand, a blue Princess phone.

"I don't know why I let them talk me into this thing," she said, picking up the phone, trying to laugh and make a joke out of something—anything to break the harshness in the air. "You can't dial it, and you can't hang it up." She sat on the edge of the bed, the phone in her lap, and held it with one hand while dialing with the other. She made a mistake on the third number and broke the connection, laughing uneasily, saying, "See what I mean?"

The second time she managed to dial the right number. Parker stood with his back against the wall, by the door, watching her.

She was answered on the third ring, and she asked for someone named Irma. Then there was a little pause, and she carefully didn't look at Parker. When Irma finally came on, she gave her the story about the twenty-dollar loan.

Irma had some questions, and she answered them. Why had she waited so late to call? Because she'd been thinking about it all evening and getting madder and madder, and finally she'd decided to call. And where did she ever meet Mal Resnick, anyway? At that party thrown for that guy Bernie from Las Vegas that time—didn't Irma remember?—when twelve of the girls were sent to the party and Mal had been there. And why had she loaned a perfect stranger twenty dollars? Because he was in the Outfit, and it seemed all right. In fact it seemed like good politics. And was her vacation over? No, not till tomorrow.

She did it well, with no hint by word or tone that anything was wrong, and at last Irma agreed to give her Mal's new address if she promised not to go around there till morning because Linda was there tonight. She promised, and then she took the pad and pencil from the nightstand and wrote down the address.

When she'd finished thanking Irma and had hung up, having trouble making the receiver stay in the cradle, she put the phone back on the night table and got to her feet, holding out the pad. "Here," she said. "The St. David Hotel on East 57th. Room 516."

He took the pad from her. "You did fine," he said.

"Go on if you're going," she said, suddenly weary. "I've got to pack."

"Pack?"

"You're going to kill him tonight," she said, her voice drained. "Tomorrow, Irma is going to remember me calling, wanting to know where he was. They'll come around, and they'll ask questions, and then they'll kill me. I've got to leave here tonight."

"Thanks," he said.

She looked at him sullenly. "Don't thank me," she said. "I didn't do it out of any love for you. If I'd refused, *you'd* have killed me. This way, I've got a few hours' head start."

6

Parker came in through the window, seeing Mal rise up, head twisting over his shoulder, face slack with panic. He saw Mal make his lunge toward the dressing gown on the chair, and knew there must be a gun in the pocket of it. But he didn't hurry. He had plenty of time now, all the time in the world.

He came across the room. Mal fell into the chair, he and the chair clattering together to the floor, and now the woman sat up, bewildered, not yet frightened, blinking at him. She raised one arm to cover her breasts.

Mal was comical, a slapstick comedian, the way he got himself all tangled up in the chair and the dressing gown. His arms flailed around, searching for the pocket where the gun was. Parker came over to him and kicked the chair out of the way, and Mal came up at last with the gun in his hand, his face still slack but his movements jerkily fast, as though he were operated by strings.

Mal came up and around with the gun in his sweaty hand, but Parker reached out and took hold of the barrel and slipped the gun right out of his hand. And the metal of the butt showed darker and gleaming from his sweat.

Parker tossed the gun away into the corner with the chair, and reached down and took Mal's neck in his hands. Mal thrashed on the floor like a fish, arms and legs pinwheeling, and Parker held his neck steady as a rock and looked over his bobbing head at the woman sitting up on the bed. "You're a pro. Keep your mouth shut, you'll walk out of here."

Her mouth had been just opening, a scream welling up in her throat, but now she forced the scream back down. She willed her mouth closed again, and sat silent, watching wide-eyed as Parker held tight to Mal's throbbing neck and Mal's arms and legs moved with increasing heaviness. And then, all at once, Parker let him go. Mal fell backward, only half-conscious, his hands coming to his throat, the breath scraping into his lungs with a sound like two pieces of dry wood scraped together.

Parker stood over him, and it was too easy. And it wasn't enough. He didn't want to torture Mal, he wouldn't have got anything from that but wasted time. Ending his life, quick and hard and with his own hands, that was the way.

But it was too easy, and it wasn't enough. For the first time he thought about the money. Half the take was his. The others were dead. He and Mal were alive; that meant half the take was his.

He wanted the money, too. Killing Mal wasn't enough, it left a hole in the world afterward. Once he'd killed that bastard, what then? He had less than two thousand dollars to his name. He had to go on living, he had to get back into his old groove. The resort hotels and the occasional job, the easy comfortable life he'd had till this bastard had come along in his taxicab and told him about the job on the island. And to get back to that life, he needed money. Half. Forty-five thousand dollars.

He said it aloud. "Forty-five thousand dollars, Mal, that's what you owe me."

Mal tried to speak, but it came out a croak. His voice wasn't working yet; the bad color hadn't completely faded from his face.

Parker looked at the woman. "Get out of here," he said. "Get dressed and get out of here."

She jumped up from the bed, clumsy with terror, and if she was normally a beautiful and graceful woman it was impossible to tell it now.

"Mal," said Parker. "Do you want her to call the police?"

"No," croaked Mal.

"Do you want her to call the Outfit?"

"No."

Parker nodded, and turned to the woman, who was bent awkwardly, stepping into her panties, cumbersome in her haste. "Listen, you," he said. "Listen to what Mal has to say."

She stopped, staring at them, and Mal croaked, "Don't talk to nobody, don't tell nobody about this. The envelope's in the living room. Take it—go home—don't say nothing to nobody."

"That's good," Parker said. He sat down on the edge of the bed, and they waited until the woman had left. Then Parker got to his feet again. "You owe me forty-five thousand dollars, Mal."

Mal thought now that maybe he wouldn't be killed after all. Maybe Parker didn't want to kill him, just to get half of the money. He struggled up from the floor, still shaky, and said, "I don't have it right now, Parker, I—"

"What did you do with it?"

"I had to pay the Outfit eighty thousand dollars. I gave it all to them."

That would do it. That would be enough. To go to the syndicate—the Outfit, whatever they wanted to call it—to go to them and get his money back. He needed that much—he needed to act, to force, to push. Mal wasn't enough, he was easy, he was too easy, he was the easiest thing that ever happened.

"All right," said Parker. "It's the same Outfit here as Chicago, right?"

Mal nodded, puzzled. "Sure. Coast to coast, Parker, it's all the same."

"Who runs it here? Here in New York, who's the boss?"

"What do you want, Parker? You can't—"

"Do you want to die, Mal?"

"What? No! For Christ's sake, Parker—"

They stood facing each other. Parker held out his hands where Mal could see them, curved, ready to fit around Mal's neck. "Who's the boss in New York, Mal?"

"*They'll* kill me, Parker, *they'll*—"

"Not if you're already dead." Parker rested his hands on Mal's neck, just easy, not squeezing yet. His arms were straight out, and this way he was unprotected should Mal decide to kick him in the groin or punch him in the stomach, but he knew Mal wouldn't try anything like that. He didn't have anything to worry about from Mal. Mal was easy.

Mal's lip quivered, and then he said, "There's two of them, Mr. Fairfax and Mr. Carter. They run things in New York, Mr. Fairfax and Mr. Carter."

"And where do I find them, Mal?"

"Mr. Fairfax isn't in town right now." Mal's tongue came out, moistening his lips, and his eyes flickered to the corner where Parker had thrown the gun.

"Parker," he said, pleading, "we can work something—"

"Where do I find Carter?"

"Please, Parker, it won't do you any good. You couldn't get in to see him anyway, and we can work—"

Parkers hands tensed and relaxed on Mal's neck. "Where do I find Carter?"

Mal hesitated, flickered his eyes, gestured with his hands, shifted his weight back and forth from leg to leg, and capitulated. "582 Fifth Avenue," he said. He closed his eyes, as though then it wouldn't really be him telling. "He's got an office there, Frederick Carter Investments. Seventh floor, I forget the number."

Parker let his hands fall away from Mal's neck. "Fine," he said. "That's fine."

Mal wanted to plead again, started to say something again about how they could work something out, but Parker stopped him. "Tell me about the office. You say I couldn't get in. Why not?"

Mal told him about the layout of the office, the silent man who came out, and what the silent man said when it was someone Mr. Carter didn't want to see.

Parker nodded, listening, and said. "You been there recently, huh, Mal? When you heard I was after you?" He looked around the room. "They threw you away, huh? They wouldn't help you?"

"They said it was up to me. Mr. Carter said so."

Parker laughed at him. "They should have known better, huh, Mal?"

Then he took Mal's neck in his hands again, and this time he didn't let go till Mal stopped breathing.

FOUR

1

*T*he silent man pulled open the unmarked door and looked out at Parker. He hesitated and then said, "Can I help you?" He sounded puzzled. He didn't recognize Parker as an Outfit man, but he didn't look like an investment customer either.

Parker said, "Tell your boss the guy who killed Mal Resnick is here."

The puzzlement on the silent man's face shifted subtly from real to fake. He said, "I'm sorry. I don't know what you're talking about."

"You don't have to," Parker said.

He turned his back and walked over to one of the sofas. Sitting down, he reached over to the table and picked up a copy of *U.S. News & World Report.* He read on the cover that the automobile industry was recovering.

The silent man stood watching him, not knowing what to do. When Parker didn't look up, he shrugged and went out and closed the door again. Parker put the magazine down and got to his feet. He studied the two fox-hunting prints on the wall, but neither were one-way mirrors. He looked at the unmarked door. The knob was a golden brass, with the keyhole set in it. It looked like a tough lock. Parker thought of three men he knew who could go through it like a knife through butter.

Five minutes went by, and the silent man came back, looking mistrustful. He said, "Mr. Carter will see you. I've got to frisk you first."

Parker raised his arms at his sides. Mal was dead now, and the mean urgency was out of him. He was reasonable now, a businessman coming to discuss a debt. The silent man could frisk him—it didn't matter.

The silent man finished and stepped back. "You're clean," he said grudgingly. He unlocked the door and led the way through. They went through the gray office and the living room–bar into Mr. Carter's office. Mr. Carter sat at his desk, reading a mimeographed stock report. He looked up and said, "I didn't know Mal was dead."

"He is."

"Oh, I don't doubt your word." He motioned at the leather chair Mal had sat in. "Sit down there."

The silent man was behind Parker. He turned away, heading for his chair in the corner, and Parker spun around, left hand extended, fingers rigid. The tips of his fingers jolted into the silent man's side, just above the belt. The silent man grunted and bent sideways, trying to breathe. Parker's right hand came across, balled in a fist, and clipped the side of his jaw, just under the ear. The silent man started to fall, and before he hit the floor Parker had the .32 out of his hip holster. He turned back and Mr. Carter was still reaching into his drawer. He stopped when he saw the .32 pointed at him.

Parker said, "Close the drawer."

Mr. Carter looked at his man on the floor and closed the drawer. Parker broke the .32 open and emptied the shells into his hand. The noses had been scored, to make them spread when they hit. He walked over to the desk and put the .32 on the green blotter. The shells rattled into the wastebasket.

"You don't want me with a gun. I don't want you with a gun either."

Mr. Carter looked at his man again. "He's one of the best."

Parker shook his head. "No, he isn't. He lulls too easy." He sat down in the leather chair. "We can talk now."

Mr. Carter smiled thinly. "I think Resnick lied to me."

"Why? What did he say?"

"He said he shot you, took your proceeds from a payroll robbery, and ran off with your wife."

"One part's a lie. My wife was the one who shot me."

"Oh? That way I can see it." Mr. Carter spread his hands palm down on the blotter, to either side of the empty gun. "There's something you want from me?"

"Mal gave you people eighty thousand dollars."

"*Paid* us. It was a debt."

"Forty-five thousand of it was mine. I want it back."

Mr. Carter's faint smile disappeared. He blinked, looked again at his man on the floor and said, "You can't be serious."

"It's my money."

"The organization was owed a certain sum," Mr. Carter said. "The organization was paid. Any debt Resnick owed you has died with him, so far as the organization is concerned. We don't undertake to settle our employees' personal debts."

Parker said, "You people have forty-five thousand dollars of my money. You'll give it to me."

Mr. Carter shook his head. "The request would never be approved. The organization would certainly decline to—"

Parker interrupted. "The funnies call it the syndicate. The goons and hustlers call it the Outfit. You call it the organization. I hope you people have fun with your words. But I don't care if you call yourselves the Red Cross, you owe me forty-five thousand dollars and you'll pay me back whether you like it or not."

Mr. Carter's cold smile came back to his lips. "Do you realize, my friend, just what you're trying to fight? Do you have any idea just how many employees are on our organization payroll, coast to coast? Just how many affiliate organizations in how many towns? How many officials we control at local and state level all across the country?"

Parker shrugged. "You're as big as the Post Office. So you've got the assets, you can pay me back my money with no trouble at all."

Mr. Carter shook his head. "I'm trying to tell you for your own good," he said, "uh—I've forgotten your name. Resnick told me but I'm sorry, it slipped my mind."

"Parker. It won't again."

The smile strengthened for just a second. "No, I don't suppose it will. All right, Parker, allow me to give you the facts of life. The organization is not unreasonable. It pays its debts, works within acceptable business ethics, and does its best to run at a profit. Except for the fact that it works outside the law, it conforms as closely as possible to the corporate concept. In other words, if you had come to me with a legitimate corporate debt, you would have no trouble. But you are asking us to reimburse you for a personal debt contracted by a former employee. No corporation in the world would agree to that, Parker, and I'm sure our organization wouldn't either."

"Mal gave you money that didn't belong to him. It belonged to me. You know that now, so you can give it back."

"In the first place," said Mr. Carter, "*I* personally couldn't give it back. That would have to be the result of a top-level decision. In the second place, I can't tell you right now that I'm so certain what that decision would be that I'm not even going to pass the request on."

"It's not a request," Parker said. Without waiting for a comment on that, he went on. "What's your job in this organization, anyway—this corporation of yours? What are you, a vice president or something?"

"You might call me a regional manager. With another gentleman—"

"Fairfax."

Mr. Carter nodded, smiling. "Resnick told you quite a bit before he died, didn't he? Yes, Mr. Fairfax. He and I manage the New York interests of the organization."

"All right, then who runs the whole thing? You said you knew what the decision would be. Who'd make the decision?"

"A committee would—"

"One man, Carter. You go up high enough, you always come to one man."

"Not exactly. Not in this case. Three men. Any one of them, actually—"

"Are any of them in New York?"

"One. But if you're asking me to call—"

"I'm not asking you to call." Parker heard movement behind

him. He got to his feet. The silent man was coming back to consciousness, doing a push-up off the floor, getting his knees beneath him. Parker heel-kicked him in the head, and he subsided. He turned back to Mr. Carter. "I'm not asking you to call," he repeated. "I'm telling you to call."

"What will you do if I refuse?"

"Kill you, and wait for Fairfax to come back to town."

Mr. Carter made a tent of his fingers and studied it. His lips pursed and relaxed, pursed and relaxed. He looked up from under his brows at Parker and said, "I believe you. And if I call, and this gentleman refuses, as I know he will?"

"I don't know," Parker told him. "Let's see what he has to say."

Mr. Carter thought about it some more. Finally he said, "Very well. You're not going to get anywhere, but I'll call." He reached for the phone and dialed. Parker watched, remembering the number. Mr. Carter waited a moment, then said, "Fred Carter to talk to your boss, sweetheart." He paused, then frowned with annoyance and said, "Tell him Fred Carter." Another pause and, with more irritation, he said, "Bronson. I want to talk to Bronson."

Parker smiled at him, but he didn't smile back.

There was a longer wait before Bronson came on the line, and then Mr. Carter said, "Fred Carter here. I'm sorry to call you about this, but there's a problem. And your secretary made me say your name. No, I didn't want to—there's someone else here. That's essentially the problem."

Parker sat listening as Mr. Carter outlined the situation. He smiled again when Mr. Carter said the money had come from a payroll robbery in Des Moines. After that, he just sat and listened.

When the story was done, there was a pause and Mr. Carter said, "I explained all that to him. He insisted I call or he'd kill me. He's already killed his ex-wife and this man Resnick, and God knows how many others."

"Nine," said Parker, though he didn't know if that was right or not.

There was more talk. Finally Mr. Carter said, "All right. Hold on." He cupped the mouthpiece. "He wants to call one of the other two, in Florida. Then he'll call us back."

Parker shook his head. "The second you hang up, he'll send an army. We do it in one phone call."

Mr. Carter relayed the information, then said to Parker, "He says in that case the answer is no."

"Let me talk to him."

"He wants to talk to you." Mr. Carter handed over the receiver.

Parker said, "How much is this guy Carter worth to you?"

The voice in his ear was harsh and angry. "What do you mean?"

"Either I get paid, or Carter is dead."

"I don't like to be threatened."

"No one does. If you say no, I'll kill Mr. Carter, and then I'll come after you. We'll let your buddy in Florida decide. And if he says no, I'll kill you and go after him."

"You can't buck the organization, you damn fool!"

"Yes or no."

Parker waited, looking at nothing, hearing only the sound of breathing on the line. At last the angry voice said: "You'll regret it. You'll never get away from us."

"Yes or no."

"No."

"Hold on a minute."

Parker put the phone down and started around the desk. Mr. Carter blinked at him, then dove for the middle desk drawer. He got it open, but Parker's hand was first on the gun.

Mr. Carter lunged up from the chair, trying to wrestle the gun away from him, and Parker shoved it hard into his belly, to muffle the sound. He pulled the trigger, and Mr. Carter slid down him, half-falling back into the chair and then rolling out of it, hitting his head on the desk as he fell the rest of the way to the floor.

Parker put the gun down and picked up the phone. "All right," he said. "He's dead. I've got your name and phone number. In five minutes I'll have your address. In twenty-four hours I'll have you in my hands. Yes or no?"

"In twenty-four hours you'll be dead! No lone man can buck the organization."

"I'll be seeing you," Parker said.

2

When Justin Fairfax walked into his parkside Fifth Avenue apartment, he had two bodyguards with him, but they were both carrying luggage. When Parker met them in the living room he already had Mr. Carter's gun in his hand. "Don't put the luggage down," he said.

Fairfax was angry anyway. His Florida vacation had been cut short by what was obviously a lot of nonsense. He glowered at Parker and demanded, "Who are you? What's the meaning of this?" The bodyguards stood flat-footed, holding the luggage. They weren't paid to be foolhardy.

Parker said, "I'm the reason you're back in New York. Stand over there by the sofa. Keep your hands where I can see them."

"You're Parker?"

"Stand over there by the sofa."

Fairfax backed cautiously to the sofa, watching Parker's face. He was looking at a man who had challenged the organization. He wanted to know what such a man would look like.

To the bodyguards, Parker said, "Turn around. Hold on to that luggage."

They turned. Being professionals, they knew what was coming. Knowing what was coming, they tensed themselves, hunching their heads low on their necks, tightening their shoulders.

Parker turned the gun around, held it by the barrel, and looped his arm over twice. The bodyguards dropped, the luggage thumping on the rug. Fairfax reached up and touched his mustache as though to reassure himself it was there.

He was a tall and stately man, graying at the temples, with a clipped pepper-and-salt mustache. An aging movie star perhaps, or an idealized casino owner. He was perhaps fifty-five or a little over and clearly spent a lot of his time being pummeled by the machinery in a gymnasium.

Parker turned the gun around again and motioned with it at the bodyguards. "Drag them into the bedroom."

Fairfax touched his mustache again, considering, and then said: "This isn't going to do you any good, Parker."

"I think it will. Do you want a bullet in the knee?"

"No."

"Then drag them into the bedroom."

The bodyguards were heavy. By the time he had dragged both of them to the nearest bedroom, Fairfax was puffing, looking more his age. There wasn't any key in the lock of the bedroom door so Parker asked for it. Fairfax said, "There's only the one key. It's in the closet door there."

"Get it. And disconnect the phone. Pull out the wires."

"I don't have to. It plugs in." He unplugged the phone and showed Parker the jack. "I don't have extensions. I have outlets for the phone in all the rooms."

"Bring the phone with you."

He knew already that the fire escape was outside the window of the other bedroom. He had Fairfax lock the door, and then the two of them went back to the living room. Parker told him to sit down and he did so, saying, "I don't understand what you're doing here. I thought you were going after Bronson."

"I'm not stupid. Is that a phone outlet there?"

"Yes."

"Plug the phone in. Call Bronson. Tell him he owes me forty-five thousand dollars. Either he pays me, or he won't have anybody left to manage the New York end."

"I can't call him. He left town."

Parker grinned. "He's a brave man. Make it a long-distance call."

"It won't do any good, Parker. He let Carter die and he'll let me die too."

"With Carter, he thought I was bluffing."

"It didn't make any difference to him." Fairfax touched his mustache again. "I don't know the full details of the case," he said. "I don't know if you should get your money or not. All I know is, Bronson said no. He won't change, not for anything. He never does."

"This time he will." Parker sat down, facing the other man. "When you call him, I want you to tell him something for me. I've worked my particular line for the last eighteen years. In that time I've worked with about a hundred different men. Among them, they've worked with just about every professional in the business. You know the business I mean."

"All I know about you," said Fairfax, his mouth hidden by the fingers against his mustache, "is that you were involved in a pay-roll robbery in Des Moines."

"That's the business I mean." Parker shifted the gun to the other hand. "There's you people with your organization, and there's us. We don't have any organization, but we're professionals. We know each other. We stick with each other. Do you know what I'm talking about?"

"Bank robbers," said Fairfax.

"Banks, payrolls, armored cars, jewelers, anyplace that's worth the risk." Parker leaned forward. "But we don't hit casinos," he said. "We don't hit layoff bookies or narcotic caches. We don't hit the syndicate. You're sitting there wide open—you can't squeal to the law, but we don't hit you."

"There's a good reason for that," said Fairfax. "We'd get you if you tried it."

Parker shook his head. "You'd never find us. We aren't organized, we're just a guy here and a guy there that know each other. You're organized, so you're easy to find."

"In other words," said Fairfax, "if we don't give you the forty-five thousand dollars, you'll steal it—is that it?"

"No. I don't do things like that. I just keep chopping off heads. But I also write letters, to those hundred men I told you about. I tell them the syndicate hit me for forty-five Gs; do me a favor and hit them back once when you've got the chance. Maybe half of them will say the hell with it. The other half are like me; they've got the job all cased. A lot of us are like that. You organized people are so wide open. We walk into a syndicate place and we look around, and just automatically we think it over—we think about it like a job. We don't do anything about it because you people are on the same side as us, but we think about it. I've walked around for years with three syndicate grabs all mapped out in my head, but I've never done anything about it. The same with a lot of the people I know. So all of a sudden they've got the green light, they've got an excuse. They'll grab for it."

"And split with you?"

"Hell, no. I'll get my money from you people, personally. They'll keep it for themselves. And they'll cost you a hell of a lot more than forty-five thousand dollars."

Fairfax rubbed his mustache with the tips of his fingers. "I don't know if that's a bluff or not," he said. "I don't know your kind. But if they're anything like the people I do know, it's a bluff. The people I know worry about their own skins, not about mine."

Parker grinned again. "I'm not saying they'd do it for me," he said. "Not because it was me. Because they've got a syndicate grab in their heads, and all they need is an excuse." He switched the gun back to his right hand. "Take your fingers down from your face."

Fairfax dropped his hand into his lap, quickly, as though touching his mustache was a habit he was trying to stop. He cleared his throat and said, "Maybe you know what you're talking about, I couldn't say."

"You can say it to Bronson." Parker motioned to the phone. "Call him now. Tell him what I told you. If he says no, you're dead and it costs him money. He'll still have to pay me sooner or later anyway."

"I'll call him," said Fairfax. "But it won't do any good."

Parker sat listening as Fairfax put in a call to Bronson at the Ravenwing Hotel, Las Vegas. It took a while because Bronson was out of his room and had to be paged, but finally he came on the phone and Fairfax gave him the setup, including Parker's threat. "I don't know if he's bluffing or not. He says they wouldn't do it out of friendship to him, but because they've wanted to hit some of our places for years anyway."

After that there was a pause, and Fairfax studied Parker as he listened. Then he said, "No, I don't think so. He's hard, that's all. Hard and determined and don't give a damn."

Parker shifted the gun to his other hand. Fairfax listened again, then extended the phone to Parker. "He wants to talk to you."

"About what?"

"Terms."

"Stand over there by the window."

Fairfax set the receiver on the table, got to his feet, and walked over to the window. From deeper in the apartment, a hammering began. Fairfax grimaced and said, "I'm replacing those two."

"It was your fault," Parker said. "Don't make your body-guards carry your suitcases." He crossed over to the sofa, sat down where Fairfax had been sitting, and put the phone to his ear. "All right, what is it?"

"You're an annoyance, Parker," said Bronson's heavy angry voice. "You're an irritation, like a mosquito. All right. Forty-five thousand dollars is chickenfeed. It's a small account, for small punks with small minds. To get rid of the mosquito, all right—I'll swat you with forty-five thousand dollars. But let me tell you something, Parker."

"Tell me, then," said Parker.

"You're a marked man. You'll get your petty payoff, and after that you're dead whether you know it or not. I'm not going to send anybody out after you especially. I wouldn't spend the time or the money. I'm just going to spread the word around. A cheap penny-ante heister named Parker, I'm going to say. If you happen to see him, make him dead. That's all, just if you happen to see him. Do you get what I'm talking about, Parker?"

"Sure," said Parker. "Carter told me all about it. You're as big as the Post Office. You're coast to coast. I should look you up in the yellow pages."

"You can't go anywhere, Parker. Not anywhere. The organization will find you."

"The organization doesn't have three men in it from coast to coast who could make me dead. Send your Mal Resnicks after me, Bronson. Send your Carters and your Fairfaxes. Send their bodyguards. You'll have to hire a lot of new people, Bronson."

"All right, bush leaguer," said Bronson angrily. "Keep talking big. Just tell me where to make the drop on your crummy forty-five thousand."

"There's a section of Brooklyn," Parker said. "Canarsie. There's a BMT subway to it. Two men, carrying the cash in a briefcase, should hit there at two o'clock tomorrow morning. I'll be on the platform. No bill over a hundred, none under a ten. If it's stuff you printed yourself, you better send two expendable men. If you send more than two, the mosquito will drain your blood."

"Talk big, Parker," said Bronson. "What's the name of this subway stop?"

"It's the end of the line."

"For you too, Parker." Bronson hung up.

Parker put the phone back on its hook and got to his feet. The pounding still echoed dully from the bedroom. Fairfax was touching his mustache with the tips of his fingers. When Parker stood up, he seemed to suddenly notice he was doing it because his hand jerked down to his side and he looked embarrassed.

Parker said, "You're lucky, Fairfax. Your boss gave in easier than I figured. And that's a pity. I would have enjoyed finishing you." Then he smiled. "Maybe he'll cross me. Maybe he'll try for an ambush. Then I'll be able to come back."

Fairfax touched his mustache. "I'm going to fire those two," he said.

Parker shook his head. "It won't do any good."

3

*M*omentum kept him rolling. He wasn't sure himself any more how much was a tough front to impress the organization and how much was himself. He knew he was hard, he knew that he worried less about emotion than other people. But he'd never enjoyed the idea of a killing. And now he wasn't sure himself whether he'd just been putting a scare into Fairfax or if he'd really meant it.

It was momentum, that was all. Eighteen years in one business, doing one or two clean fast simple operations a year, living relaxed and easy in the resort hotels the rest of the time with a woman he liked, and then all of a sudden it all got twisted around. The woman was gone, the pattern was gone, the relaxation was gone, the clean swiftness was gone.

He spent months as a vag in a prison farm; he spent over a month coming across the country like an O. Henry tramp; he devoted time and effort and thought on an operation that wasn't clean or fast or simple and that didn't net him a dime—the finding and killing of Mal Resnick. And more killing, and bucking the syndicate more for the mean hell of it than anything else, as though for eighteen years he'd been storing up all the meanness, all the viciousness, and now it had to come rushing out.

He didn't know if he was going to make it, if he was going to hold up the syndicate and get away with it, and he didn't really care. He was doing it, and rolling along with the momentum, and that was all that mattered.

And now, another killing. He stood leaning against a tree, in the darkness of Farragut Avenue, looking at the shack housing Stegman's cab company, waiting for Stegman to come back out. Stegman had lied: he'd known how to get in touch with Mal. He *had* gotten in touch with Mal. There wasn't any other way Mal could have gotten spooked that way.

So there was now a debt to settle with Stegman, too. That was the whole difference right there. From the easy known pattern to this new pattern, collecting on debts. Mal owed him, Lynn owed him, the syndicate owed him, Stegman owed him. He was owed; he collected. It was a new pattern, but it would be good to run at last to the end of it and get back to the old one again.

He'd have to find another Lynn. There were plenty of them, around the resort-hotel swimming pools. And this time he'd know to watch her a little closer, and not to fall in love.

It was after midnight. If Stegman didn't show pretty soon, he'd have to wait till after the payoff. Stegman was in there now with his poker cronies. Parker had watched them troop in, had seen the light go on in back, and now they were playing poker. But the game had to end sometime.

Parker had walked a block to a luncheonette around ten o'clock for a hamburger and coffee, and when he'd come back the light was still on back there, the players' cars were still parked on Farragut Avenue: the game was still in progress.

Parker lit another cigarette and walked around the tree. There were trees on both sides of the street out here, and private homes, one or two families. It was like a town somewhere, or the residential part of a medium-sized city. It wasn't like New York at all.

Parker walked around the tree and looked down the block into the darkness where the teenaged couple had walked half an hour ago. They'd gone up onto a porch and a glider had squeaked for a while, and now it was quiet. They couldn't see him, and he couldn't see them.

Everybody had a pattern. They had a pattern too, a quiet simple pattern, but it would change. He had a pattern, a messy complicated pattern, but it would change. Soon, now.

The door of the shack opened and the poker players came out. Parker strolled down the block, away from the shack, looking over his shoulder. Stegman stood in the doorway a minute, talking to two of them, and then went back into the shack. The rear room lights stayed on. The poker players got into their cars and drove away.

A cab pulled up, and the driver went into the shack, and then came right back out again and into his car and drove off. There was a radio operator in the front room, Stegman in the back room, and that was all.

Parker walked across the street. He went around to the back and looked through the window. Stegman sat at the table, dealing out poker hands, making imaginary bets. He must have lost tonight.

Parker went around front again. The radio operator sat at his board, reading a paperback book. Parker went in and showed the radio operator his gun, and said, "Be very quiet now."

It was a different operator from last time.

"We don't have any dough here," the radioman said. "It isn't kept here."

"Just be quiet," Parker told him. He went over to the other door and opened it. "Come on out, Stegman."

Stegman jumped, the cards falling out of his hands. "Oh my God," he said. "Oh my God."

"You'll see Him soon," Parker said. "Come on out here." He motioned with the gun.

Stegman came out, trembling, unsteady on his feet. Lies quivered on his lips, but he didn't tell any of them.

Parker stood behind him. "We're going for a ride," he said. "We'll take the same car as last time." He prodded Stegman in the small of the back with the gun.

They went out to the car. Stegman slid behind the wheel, and looked at the radio under the dashboard, licking his lips. Parker said, "Do you think he's calling the cops? Or maybe the other drivers. Turn it on, let's hear what he's saying."

Stegman switched the radio on. His fingers were damp with sweat: he had trouble turning the knob. Only static came from the radio, so the operator must have been on the phone instead, calling the police.

"We'll go that way," said Parker, pointing with the gun toward Rockaway Parkway.

Stegman started the car. He stalled it right away because his foot was nervous on the clutch. The second time, he got it moving. They bumped over the sidewalk to the street and drove across Rockaway Parkway into the darkness on the other side.

Parker said, "Make the first left."

Stegman made the left, onto East 96th Street, a side street off a side street, somnolent and dark, and Parker said, "Pull over to the curb. Turn the engine off."

Stegman did as he was told. Parker put the gun in his lap and rabbit-punched Stegman in the Adam's apple. Stegman gasped, his head ducking forward, chin tucked against his chest, and he gurgled when he tried to breathe.

"You told me no more favors," Parker reminded him. "You should have meant it." He grabbed Stegman by the hair and rammed his face into the steering wheel. Then he rabbit-punched again, the side of his hand slicing up, jolting into the underpart of Stegman's nose, snapping his head back. Hard enough, that meant blinding pain. A little harder, it meant death. This wasn't quite hard enough to kill.

Stegman moaned, spittle bubbling at the corners of his mouth. Parker was suddenly disgusted. He didn't want any more of this, only to get it over. He picked up the gun by the barrel, swung four times, and Stegman was dead.

Parker wiped the gun butt on Stegman's coat and got out of the car. He tucked the gun in under his belt and walked the rest of the way down the block to Glenwood Road and up to Rockaway Parkway and across the street to the subway entrance.

This was a strange stretch of subway, neither subway nor el. The tracks rode at ground level, with the station platform like a commuter-town railroad depot, except that the tracks came only as far as this platform, one set on either side, and then stopped. End of the line.

Off to the right were the yards, lined with strings of grimy subway cars. Beyond were new row houses, brick, two stories high, where the cab drivers lived, and farther away a bulky city project, seven stories high, where the elevator operators lived. The land was flat out here, all flat.

Two trains flanked the platform now, their doors open. A lit sign under the platform's shed roof said NEXT TRAIN, with an arrow pointing to the left. A heavy man in a corduroy jacket sat on the platform bench, reading the *News,* with a lunch bucket beside him.

Parker went over and sat next to the man. He picked up the lunch bucket and snapped it open and looked at the Luger nestled inside. The man dropped his *News* and reached for the bucket.

Parker shook his head, put the bucket on the bench on the side away from the Outfit man, and said, "You better get on your train before it pulls out."

The man looked back toward the turnstiles and the change booth and the rest rooms, then shrugged and got to his feet. He folded his paper and put it under his arm and stepped onto the train.

Parker stood and walked down the platform, carrying the lunch bucket. The rest rooms were in a little separate clapboard shack on the platform, beyond the end of the tracks. There was an anteroom with a radiator, for waiting in wintertime, and the two green doors.

Parker went on into the men's room. Two cowboys in flannel shirts and khaki pants stood there, doing nothing. Their shirttails hung outside their pants.

Parker opened the lunch bucket and took the Luger out and showed it to them. "Take off your shirts," he said. "Don't reach under them."

One started to do it, but the other one blinked and smiled and said, "What's going on?"

Parker waited, ignoring the opening. The one who had started on the top button hesitated, looking at his partner. The partner's smile flickered and he said, "I don't know what you want, buddy. What's the problem?"

"No problem," Parker told him. "Take off your shirt."

"But I don't want to take off my shirt."

"I'll pull the trigger when the train starts," Parker told him. "If you want noise before that, jump me."

The hesitant one said, "The hell with it. Do like he says, Artie. What's the percentages?"

Artie considered, and shrugged, and started unbuttoning his shirt. They took off their shirts and stood holding them in their hands. They each had two small revolvers tucked into their trousers, in under their belts.

Parker said, "Turn around." They did so, and he reached around them, taking the guns away, putting them in the sink. Then he said, "Your train's going to leave in a minute. Better hurry."

They put their shirts back on wordlessly and left the room. Parker dropped the four guns in a water closet and went back outside. He walked along the train that was to leave next and saw the two cowboys with the man in the corduroy jacket. The three were sitting hunched together, talking. They looked up and watched him go by.

Down at the other end of the platform was the dispatcher's building, tall and narrow. Beside it was a Coke machine, and a man in a business suit carrying a briefcase and holding a bottle of Coke. He'd been there when Parker had put his token in the turnstile, and he was still there. Parker hadn't yet seen him drink any of the Coke. He was looking out toward the trains in the yards.

Parker walked the length of the platform and stopped by the Coke machine. He said, "You got change of a quarter?"

"Of course," said the man. He put his bottle of warm Coke on top of the machine, switched the briefcase to his other hand, and reached into his trouser pocket.

Parker opened the lunch bucket and took the Luger out. His back was to the platform. He said, "Show me what's in your briefcase."

"Of course," the man said again. He seemed unsurprised. He released the two straps and turned the flap back. He started to reach inside, and Parker shook his head. The man smiled and pulled the briefcase lips apart instead. There was a long-barreled .25 target pistol inside.

"Close it up again," Parker said. The man did so. "Put it down beside the machine, and go get on your train."

He watched as the man walked down the platform and got on the same car as the other three. A few minutes later, the conductor and the engineer clattered down the metal outside staircase from the second floor of the dispatcher's building and boarded the train.

The doors slid shut and the train pulled out. The lit sign switched, showing that the train on the other side was now next.

Half an hour later, at twenty past one, five more of them arrived, wearing flashy suits and carrying musical instrument cases. They got off their train and stood around laughing and talking loudly, and Parker waited for ten minutes by the Coke machine, wanting to be sure. When they still had made no move to leave, he was sure.

He went over and introduced himself and said, "You better hurry if you want to make your gig. Or you can make your play instead, right now."

The other four looked at the one with the trombone case. That one looked at the train beside him, with the people on it, and the woman in the distant change booth, and the dispatcher's building. Their car wasn't outside yet, so they didn't make their play.

At quarter to two, a woman got off a train and left an overnight bag on the platform bench. Parker caught up with her and gave her the bag back. She looked frightened when he handed it to her and hurried away toward the street.

When she left, Parker went into the phone booth on the platform and called Fairfax's apartment. Fairfax answered, and Parker recognized the voice. He said, "I just got rid of the woman with the overnight bag. I haven't killed any of these jokers yet, but the next one I will. And if the money doesn't show, I'll come back for you."

Fairfax said, "Just a moment." The line hummed for a little, and then Fairfax came back on. "It'll be a little late."

"That's all right," said Parker.

There weren't any more of them. At twenty to three, a train pulled in and two men got off it together, one carrying a suitcase. They came over to Parker, sitting on the bench, and put the suitcase down on the bench beside him. They started away again, without a word, but Parker said, "Wait."

They turned around and he motioned at the suitcase. "Open it."

They looked at each other and licked their lips. They didn't know if it was bugged or not. Finally, one of them opened the two catches and lifted the top. There was nothing inside but money.

They sighed with relief, and Parker said, "Fine. Close it again." They did so, and walked away down the platform and through the exit and out to the street.

There were three ways away from here. There was the subway. There was the bus that came in at the end of the platform by the turnstiles, free transfer from and to the subway. There was the exit and the walk to the street. They would be ready for him whichever way he went.

He walked down by the Coke machine and set the suitcase down. He transferred the Luger from the lunch bucket to his side pants pocket and the target pistol from the briefcase to under his belt by the right hip pocket. He still had Mr. Carter's pistol, and this he held in his left hand.

He picked up the suitcase again, walked to the outer end of the platform and down the steps past the sign saying TRANSIT EMPLOYEES ONLY. There was a wooden strip raised over the third rail.

Parker stepped carefully over this and over the track and toward the yards. It was dark out here and no one paid any attention to him.

He moved carefully across the yard, stepping high over each third rail, not wanting even to touch the wooden cover, and finally got past them all to a wide grass-grown gravel driveway. There was more light here, along the driveway, and he walked carefully, keeping to the darkest side. Glenwood Road was ahead, with cars parked along it and the row of houses stretching away down the cross streets. He couldn't see if there was anyone in the cars.

The driveway went through an opening in the fence around the yard. Parker paused at the fence, watched, listened, then stepped through and turned left, away from Rockaway Parkway and the subway entrance. The suitcase was heavy in his right hand, the pistol comforting in his left, held close against his side.

He crossed the street, because three colored boys were walking in his direction on this side, wearing raincoats and porkpie hats and singing in falsetto. He went on down two blocks and turned right where the project began, and tossed Mr. Carter's gun into a litter basket. Whoever fished it out in this neighborhood, it would be a long while before it got to the law.

He transferred the suitcase to his left hand, and walked along with his right hand close to the Luger in his pants pocket. A car squealed around the corner behind him, headed his way.

There was a bulldozed field to his right, where the row houses hadn't been put in yet. He ducked across that, pulling the Luger out of his pocket, and somebody in the car fired too early. He dropped to the ground, and the car raced on, screaming around the far corner and away.

He got to his feet and strode deeper across the field. A high wooden wall separated the field from the backyards of row houses facing on the next street. He crouched down by the wall, the Luger in his hand, and waited.

The same car came around the block again, moving more slowly now, and stopped opposite him. He was in pitch blackness against the wall and couldn't be seen. After a minute, the back door of the car opened and two men got out. They strolled across the field to where he had dropped, wandered around in a small circle, and strolled back.

They stood by the car, and after a minute two more cars came down the street and parked. Men got out of them, and they had a conference. Then two of the cars took off again, going down to the corner, at Flatlands Avenue, both moving slowly. One turned right, and the other turned left.

The third car stayed where it was. Three men got out of it and strolled across the street to the project and disappeared in the darkness among the buildings. The driver stayed in the car, his cigarette glowing faintly from time to time, and watched the field.

Parker moved along the fence back to Glenwood Road, leaving the suitcase behind. The Luger was in his right hand, the target pistol in his left. He kept his hands close to his body as he moved. When he got to Glenwood Road, he stepped out onto the sidewalk and started to whistle.

He walked along, still whistling, and turned at the corner and walked down the block toward the car. The driver watched him in the rearview mirror, but he wasn't carrying a suitcase, and he was whistling.

The car window was open. When Parker reached it, he turned and set both gun barrels on the sill, pointing at the driver, and murmured, "One word."

The driver froze, both hands clenched on the wheel.

Parker said, "Slide over and get out on this side." He stepped back, and the driver obeyed. "Now walk out across the field there."

The two of them walked back to where he'd left the suitcase. He reversed the Luger and swung it, and the driver went down.

He left the target pistol with him, picked up the suitcase, and hurried back to the car.

He slid in, started the engine, and roared away. As he was turning the corner, a man came running out from one of the project buildings half a block back.

He parked the car off Flatbush Avenue near Grand Army Plaza and took a cab into Manhattan.

4

On the bed were sixteen hundred slips of green paper, banded in stacks of fifty. There were twenty stacks marked *ten*, ten stacks marked *fifty*, two stacks marked *one hundred.* The numbers on all the slips of paper added up to forty-five thousand.

Parker sat on the chair beside the bed and looked at the money. The suitcase, empty now, lay on the floor at his feet. He had counted the money and it was all there, and now he sat and looked at it and wondered how he had happened to get it.

But it wasn't really that hard to figure out. He could follow Bronson's reasoning with no trouble at all. There was this mosquito, this Parker, causing trouble and disruptions. He wants forty-five thousand dollars. All right, give him the forty-five thousand dollars.

Try to get him when the delivery is made, but if you don't get him the hell with it, he's got forty-five thousand dollars. So then he won't cause any more trouble and disruptions. And the organization has all the time and all the facilities to get him later on. He won't be bothering the organization any more, and the organization can take care of him at its leisure. Forty-five thousand isn't so much, when you consider the benefits.

So. That was Bronson's side. His own side was simple, too; he had eighteen years of a pattern, and the pattern had been ripped apart. One job, the island job, had gone wrong and ripped the pattern apart. Now they were both dead, Lynn and Mal, the two who had done it to him. And he had made the job right again by getting his share back. He couldn't go back to the pattern while that one job was still wrong.

Now he could go back. He had money to last him two or three years of the old life, and a plastic surgery. He'd have to go out to Omaha, to Joe Sheer, and find out the name of that doctor that had done the job on him. That was when Joe had retired, three years ago. He'd had his face changed because you never knew when you'd run into somebody who saw your face on a job ten years ago and still remembered.

With a new face, with forty-five thousand dollars, the organization could look forever and never find him. He'd have to be a little more careful than before about the people he worked with on jobs, but that was no problem. He liked to pick and choose his jobs and his partners anyway.

A job had soured and now it was straight again. It was as simple as that.

He roused himself, putting out his cigarette, and picked up the suitcase from the floor. He carefully packed the bundles of money back into it, closed it, slid it under his bed. Then he picked up the phone and asked for American Airlines, and made a reservation on the 3:26 P.M. plane for Omaha.

After that he left a call for noon, took a leisurely shower, and opened the pint of vodka he'd bought on the way back. He could drink it now; he was finished and he could relax. In Omaha, maybe Joe could set him up with a woman. If not, it could wait till Miami.

He woke to the jangling of the telephone, telling him it was noon, the first day of the new-old pattern. The hotel wasn't as good as he was used to, but it didn't matter. He was on his way back, starting now.

He took another shower, and dressed, and packed. He left the room carrying the two suitcases, his own and the one full of money. He rode down in the elevator and started across the lobby, and the desk clerk pointed him out to two men in rumpled suits.

They came toward him, and he hesitated, not believing they'd dare try anything here. And how could they find him here anyway? They couldn't. But he was unarmed, the Luger thrown away last night on Flatbush Avenue.

The two men came over, and one reached to his hip pocket, and Parker tensed, ready to throw the suitcase with the clothing in it. But all that came out of the pocket was a wallet. It flipped open, showing the badge pinned to the leather. The owner of the wallet said, "Mr. Edward Johnson?"

What is this? What is this? "Yes," he said, because the desk clerk had pointed him out. "What is it?"

"We want to talk to you." The plainclothesman looked around at the lobby. "In private," he said. "We'll go to the manager's office."

"What is it? What's it all about?"

"There are some questions. If you'll come with us?"

One of them had his left arm, gently. It was only to the manager's office, so he didn't fight it. He didn't try to guess what it was all about. He went along, ready, waiting to find out the score before making any kind of move.

The three employees behind the desk watched out of the corners of their eyes as the detectives took him through a door marked *Private* into a small empty office. The door to the next room, the manager's office, was open, and the manager peered at them from his desk.

One of the detectives went over and said through the door, "We won't be long, sir. Thank you for your cooperation."

"That's perfectly all right," the manager said. He seemed embarrassed.

The detective smiled and closed the door. Then he turned the smile off again and said, "Sit down, Mr. Johnson."

Parker sat down on the corner of the sofa nearest the door, ready, waiting for them to tell him what it was all about.

The silent one stood by the door. The other one pulled a chair over and sat on it backwards, facing Parker, his forearms folded on the chair back, his bent knees jutting out at the sides.

"Two days ago," he said, "you were in a grocery store on West 104th Street between Central Park West and Manhattan Avenue. You spent some time in the back room of the store, talking with Manuel Delgardo, the proprietor. When two patrolmen entered the store, you stated that you were having a soft drink with Mr. Delgardo in the back of the store, and that you were there looking for Mr. Delgardo's son, Jimmy. You stated that you and Jimmy Delgardo once worked for the same trucking company in Buffalo. You also brought up the subject of narcotics, although neither of the patrolmen had given any indication that they were thinking of narcotics or suspected you of having anything to do with junk. Is this all substantially correct, as you remember it?"

"Yes," said Parker. *Don't explain, don't justify, don't argue. Wait till you find out the score.*

The detective nodded. "Fine," he said. "Now, you also stated that you were recently laid off from a General Electric Company plant on Long Island. Is that correct?"

"That's what I said," Parker answered.

The detective caught it. "But is it correct?"

So they'd checked that part. Change stories. "No," said Parker.

The detective nodded again. "That's right, we checked you out. The California address you gave the hotel is also incorrect, isn't it?"

"Yes."

"Would you like to explain those lies?"

"You've got to give a cop a background," said Parker. "You tell him you're just drifting, he pulls you in on general principles. You give him some kind of background, he leaves you alone. Same with the hotel. I put down no permanent address, then I get a lot of static from the hotel."

"I see." The detective nodded once more. "Then the truth is that you're a drifter, that you don't really have any background or address or job or anything else, is that it?"

"That's right."

"And where did you get the money to afford this hotel?"

"I won it in a crap game."

"Where?"

Parker shook his head.

The detective reddened. "Don't shake your head at me, punk! There wasn't any crap game!"

Parker waited, ready. There wasn't any reason to do anything yet. Maybe later he'd have to pay this one back for the bad name.

The detective controlled himself. "All right," he said. "Get on your feet. Turn around. Touch the wall over the sofa, palms of your hands."

The other detective came over from the door and emptied his pockets. Then they let him sit down again.

The first one looked at his driver's license. He looked at it more closely than anyone had before, and frowned. He turned it over, and studied different parts of it, and then he licked the ball of his thumb and rubbed it against the state seal. He looked up at his partner and grinned. "A phony," he said. "Not even a good one. Here, look."

The other detective looked at the license and chuckled over it too, then handed it back. The first cop offered it to Parker, saying, "Want it back, Mr. Johnson?"

"No, thanks," said Parker. "You spoiled it."

"I'm sorry about that. What trucking firm in Buffalo did you and Jimmy Delgardo work for together?"

Parker grabbed a name out of the air. "Lester Brothers."

The detective took a notebook out of his pocket, opened it, read something, and shook his head. "Wrong."

Parker said, "Do you mind telling me what it's all about?"

"I don't mind at all," said the detective. "Because then *you'll* tell *me* what it's all about. A man interested in narcotics, like you."

"Wrong," Parker said.

"Jimmy Delgardo," said the detective, "was picked up at the

Canadian border this morning at five o'clock coming down from Montreal. He was trying to enter the United States with a carload of liquor and marijuana." He smiled from his corner of the web. "Now, Mr. Johnson," he said, "you tell me what it's all about. You tell me what your right name is and what you do for a living and what connection you have with that carload Jimmy Delgardo was driving into this country."

Parker clasped his hands behind his head and leaned back on the sofa. He started to cross one leg over the other, but instead rammed his heel into the detective's face, just above the nose. Detective and chair clattered over backward, and Parker surged out of the sofa, coming in low on the other one, who was pawing at his hip for his gun. Parker butted him in the stomach and brought his head up sharply, the crown cracking into the detective's chin. His fist came up after, catching him in the throat.

Parker stepped back, yanking the detective by the tie. The detective stumbled, falling away from the door, and Parker grabbed the suitcase full of money, pulled open the door, and ran.

As he hit the revolving door, there were shouts behind him. The glass of the door starred, higher than his head, and something tugged at the shoulder of his coat.

He got through to the street, and there was a cab waiting at the backstand outside the hotel, waiting for a fare. He pulled open the door, tossed the suitcase in and dove in after it. "Grand Central!" he shouted. "A fin if I make my train!"

There wasn't time now to get to Idlewild. The alarm would be out first.

"We're off!" cried the driver. They jolted away from the curb, squealed around the corner as the light was turning red, and weaved erratically through the traffic. Parker reached up with his left hand to touch his right shoulder. The coat was ripped there, by the seam, but the bullet hadn't touched him.

He reached out and patted the suitcase, and it was the wrong one. He looked at it, and turned his head to look out the back window. The detectives had the suitcase with the forty-five thousand. He had the suitcase with the socks and the shirts.

The cabby said, "What time's your train?"

"It just left," said Parker.

"Jeez," said the cabby. "You didn't leave yourself no time at all."

"I was kidding. There's still time." Parker smiled, showing his teeth, thinking, What do I do now? Go to the Mayor of the City of New York? Tell him the city owes me forty-five Gs?

When the cab stopped, he gave the driver a ten. He dragged the suitcase along into Grand Central Station. The clock over the rotunda said 12:53. He walked along the gates, looking at the times of departure until he came to one that said 12:58.

One of the places it was going was Albany. He went through the gate and down along the concrete platform. He said to the conductor standing by the entrance to the first passenger car, "I didn't have time to buy a ticket. I'll get it on the train."

"Wait here."

He stood there, watching back to where the cops would come if they came, and five minutes occurred one by one. Then the conductor let him board the train and asked where he wanted a ticket for.

He said, "Albany," and the conductor wrote interminably on ticket and papers, accepted his money and allowed him to go sit down.

The car was nearly empty.

He dropped into the first seat he came to, the wrong suitcase next to him, and thought about Omaha and Joe Sheer and the plastic surgeon. He'd need dough for the plastic surgeon. He had less than two thousand. He could cool at Joe Sheer's for a while, and then he'd have to make a grab.

Maybe a syndicate operation? One more bite from the mosquito before the face-change? It was the syndicate's fault that he didn't have the forty-five thousand. They did a sloppy smuggling job, and Parker got hit by a bum peg, and now the forty-five thousand was baffling the boys in the narcotics squad.

Yeah, a syndicate grab. He liked the idea.

He got off the train at Albany and went out to the airport and bought a ticket to Omaha.

5

*P*arker and the other three men came out of the elevator and walked slowly down the hall to the left. Two women were walking toward them, with furs over their shoulders and purses hanging from their forearms. As they went by, they were talking about hair rinses. They went on to the elevators and punched the down button.

Parker said softly, "Wait'll they go."

The four of them ambled along, past the door they wanted. It said St. Louis Sales, Inc. on it. The city was right, but the rest was wrong. About half of the comeback money from the St. Louis bookies came through here.

They reached the end of the hall and stood by the office door there, a typewriter company's representative, until the two women got on an elevator. Then the three men took Huckleberry Hound masks from inside their coats and put them on. Parker didn't bother; his share of this job was going for a new face anyway.

They went back down the hall, moving faster now, toward the

door marked St. Louis Sales, Inc. The man named Wiss took a chisel from his pocket and held it by the blade end, like a club. He was the only one Parker hadn't known before; Joe Sheer had recommended him. The other two, Elkins and Wymerpaugh, Parker had worked with in the past.

They stopped, flanking the door, two on either side. Parker and Elkins had guns in their hands now. Wiss hit the door glass with the chisel handle and it shattered inward, making a racket. Before the echoes had died down, he'd thrown the chisel into the room, to give them something else to think about inside, and reached through the opening to the doorknob. He pushed, and Parker and Elkins crowded in, guns first.

The three men in the small office froze. The one by the adding machine just sat there, fingers poised over the keys, staring. The one who'd been standing by the airshaft window was stopped with one hand up under his arm, the gun half-drawn from its holster. The one who'd been sitting at the other desk kept his hand in the drawer he'd opened when the glass broke.

Parker said, "Hands up and empty."

Wiss, pulling his gun, ran across the room and jerked open the door to the inner office, but it was empty. He turned back, saying, "The wheel's away!"

"Lunch," said Parker. "Let's get out before he comes back."

Wymerpaugh, standing by the doorway and watching down the hall toward the elevators, handed the briefcase to Elkins. Elkins went over to the guy at the adding machine and said, "Up."

With his hands still in the air, the adding machine man got to his feet and backed away from the desk. Elkins pulled open the typewriter well and stuffed the stacks of bills hidden in it into the briefcase. Then he gave the briefcase back to Wymerpaugh, took the other briefcase from Parker, and went through to the inside office. Wiss followed him, dragging more tools from his pockets.

The guy by the airshaft window said, "You guys are crazy. That's Outfit money."

Parker smiled thinly. "Was it?"

From the inner office there came small sounds, as Wiss and Elkins worked on the safe. Wymerpaugh closed the door and bent to peer down the hall through the hole in the glass.

Elkins and Wiss came back. Wiss was stuffing tools into his pockets and Elkins was carrying a bulging briefcase. Parker said to the guy by the airshaft window, "You know who Bronson is?"

The guy shrugged. "I've heard of a guy by that name. Back east."

"That's him. Tell him it was Parker. Tell him the mosquito decided he wanted interest on the loan. You got that?"

"It don't matter to me."

Elkins gave Parker back the briefcase, then went around and collected all the guns that had been in the office and threw them down the airshaft. Then he said, "Sit tight a few minutes, girls."

The four of them went out and down the hall toward the elevators. Wiss and Elkins and Wymerpaugh pulled off their Huckleberry Hound masks. They went past the elevators and through the door marked STAIRWELL. They went up two flights and out into the hall there and down to the lawyer's office: HERBERT LANSING, ATTORNEY-AT-LAW. Elkins unlocked the door, and they went inside.

That was the beautiful part, this office. Parker had worked it out. Somewhere in an office building this size, he'd figured, there's got to be at least one one-man office where the boss takes an occasional vacation. All they had to do was know what was going on in the building, and wait.

When Herbert Lansing took his vacation, Elkins found out about it from the elevator boy, who was lately his drinking buddy. One trip by Elkins and Wiss, in workclothes, to dummy up a key, and they were ready.

They went inside, and Elkins broke out the bottle of blended whiskey he'd stashed here when they'd made the key. They passed the bottle around, then unloaded the briefcases on the lawyer's desk and made the divvy. Parker's third—it was his case—came to just over twenty-three thousand.

He stowed it back in his briefcase, took another swig from the bottle, and sat back grinning. It all worked out fine. He was back in the groove again.

Wymerpaugh broke out a deck of cards and they played poker till four-thirty. By then Parker had closer to twenty-seven thousand. The four of them cleaned the office up, locked the door, and separated, each going to different floors.

Parker took a cab out to the Lambert–St. Louis airport and caught a six-o-five plane for Omaha. A new face now, and the old pattern. He looked out the window and smiled. Miami should be fine this time of year. Or maybe he'd go on down to the Keys.

NOV 2011

CPSIA information can be obtained at www.ICGtesting.com
Printed in the USA
LVOW061510141111

254925LV00001B/61/P

9 780446 674645